THE WOMAN IN THE PORTRAIT

This selection first published in 2024 by Cipher Press

203 Ryan House
12 Smeed Road
London, E3 2PE

Paperback ISBN: 978-1-917008-02-0
eBook ISBN: 978-1-917008-03-7

Printed and bound in the UK by TJ Books, Padstow, Cornwall

Distributed by Turnaround Publisher Services

Edited by Jack Thompson
Cover Design by Wolf Murphy-Merrydew
Typeset by Laura Jones-Rivera
Proofread by Liam Konemann

www.cipherpress.co.uk

Supported using public funding by
**ARTS COUNCIL
ENGLAND**

LOTTERY FUNDED

THE WOMAN IN THE PORTRAIT

COLLECTED SHORT STORIES
2008-2024

Juliet Jacques

Cipher
press

CONTENTS

I'M TOO SAD TO TELL YOU ABOUT *I'M TOO SAD TO TELL YOU*

Sometimes, journalists call me and beg me to tell them about Bas Jan Ader. I've always told them it's too sad to talk about, but as time has passed, they've become more persistent, so I've decided to tell you about *I'm Too Sad to Tell You*. But this is the last time.

★

I studied with Bas Jan in Los Angeles. A few years after we graduated, he invited me to his studio. He arrived as I did, camera in hand, and led me inside. He handed me the camera, stood against the wall and started weeping. I turned on the camera and pointed the lens at him.

After three minutes and twenty-two seconds, the 16mm film ran out. Immediately, the tears stopped, the last one rolling off his cheek the moment the film finished.

I put the cap back on the lens and turned to leave. He tapped me on the shoulder, led me to a café, bought me coffee and sat down.

"Did you walk here?" he asked. I nodded. "You saw anti-war protesters everywhere, yes?"

I nodded again.

"Why?"

"Well… they believe America has no right to be in Vietnam," I replied. "And they're angry about the senseless loss of life."

"You've read the papers," said Bas Jan. "They've misunderstood – perhaps deliberately. The war stimulates their anger, but it doesn't generate it. Intellectually, the protestors think the war is wrong, but their protest provides an outlet for emotions that they aren't allowed to express. The fundamental emotion is sadness – the most painful feeling, and the hardest to comprehend. People feel angry because they can't understand their sadness – the way society shuns those who make it explicit means they have to repress it, and it becomes anger."

"So why isn't everyone out protesting?"

"Because people act on their anger in different ways. Some people protest against wars; others make them. Some don't express the anger at all – they feel they're not allowed to express anger any more than sadness – and they become depressed. That's why we've made this film."

"Won't it make people more depressed?"

"No. It will make people reconnect with the raw emotion they repressed as they became adults, and force them to confront it."

"Why not challenge them with happiness?" I said. "The happiness we all felt in our childhoods."

"The happiness we claim to *remember* from our childhoods," he replied. "I think that before people can even contemplate happiness, they have to understand their sadness."

"People will say the film is too much for them."

"They will become ready."

"You think you're Christ."

"I'm not dying for anyone!" he declared. "I just make films."

"How will people know you're not faking it?"

Bas Jan stood, without looking at me, took his camera and left. I didn't call him: I heard nothing from him for several years, until I heard that *I'm Too Sad to Tell You* was part of his exhibition at the Copley Gallery in Los Angeles. Bas Jan's handwritten title flashed silently across the frame, then for the next three minutes and twenty-two seconds, his head rolled in genuine anguish, tears streaming down his cheeks.

I felt a tap on my shoulder.

"You're crying," said Bas Jan.

"You made me."

"My next work will make you happy," he said. "Come to my studio tomorrow."

★

The door was open when I arrived.

"You inspired me this," said Bas Jan as I cast my eyes upon the boat that dominated his tiny studio. "This is the *Ocean Wave*. It's the only tangible part of my next project, '*In Search of the Miraculous*'. You think it's very small. It is – only 12 and a half feet. But when I sail from Cape Cod in Massachusetts to Falmouth in England, it will become the smallest craft ever to cross the Atlantic."

"That's insane!"

"The project will hopefully contain elements of what some might consider insanity. The mental voyage is far more important than the physical one. Amidst the calmness of the ocean, without any distractions, my mind shall be focused on attacking the roots of human sadness, until it can only collapse and give way to happiness."

"How do you propose to do that?"

"By focusing upon nothing else, until I've found the answer," he said. "The journey I record in my logbooks shall be purely psychological. When I return to land, I shall publish them. They will show the way."

"You imagine yourself finding a universal formula for endless happiness?"

"Of course not! I hope to find happiness for myself, within myself. It's up to other people whether or not they follow my example."

"It's too much for you," I said. "You'll go mad."

"It's an experiment. If I fail, I fail."

You think you're Christ, I thought, but I didn't repeat myself. I shook his hand, wished him luck and said goodbye.

★

The telegram arrived as I was alone in my flat, half-watching a family strive to win thousands of dollars on a quiz show.

EMOTIONAL PATTERNS ESTABLISHED BEFORE CONS-CIOUS MEMORY STOP SO THE FIRST STEP IS THE ONLY STEP STOP ACCEPTANCE OF SADNESS IS VICTORY OVER SADNESS STOP HUMANS LOOK FOR HAPPINESS WHEN THEY SHOULD BE SEEKING CONTENTMENT STOP THE MIRACULOUS HAS BEEN FOUND AND THE SEARCH CAN STOP

The *Ocean Wave* was found by a Spanish fishing trawler, drifting off the coast of Ireland, nine months and two weeks after I received the telegram. They never found Bas Jan Ader, or his notebooks, and I never found out from where he sent his telegram. When I heard about his disappearance, I sent a copy of it to several national newspapers, all of which said that Bas Jan was not famous enough for them to publish it, especially as its content might upset emotionally fragile readers. Since then, I have kept it in a box with the paintings that I have been unable to sell, and it's too sad to show it to anyone.

'NAZIMOVA'

Statutory Declaration
Gender Recognition Act 2004

"I _____ do solemnly and sincerely declare that:

1. I am over 18 years of age.

2. I have lived as a male / female (delete word that does not apply) throughout the period of _____ years since I transitioned in _____ (month and year of transition).

3. I intend to live as a male / female (delete word that does not apply) until death.

★

I held my pen over my Gender Recognition Certificate application, contemplating my final step in moving from 'male' to 'female'.

Looking at the space where my name was supposed to go, I thought about how I'd changed mine. Coming out as transsexual, overwhelmed by friends concerned that it would ruin my life and worrying about how my parents would respond to my renouncing the name they gave me, I'd chosen as conservatively as possible, changing a few

7

letters in legally feminising it and insisting that people still call me what they always had.

How *colourless*, I thought, staring at the grey box. I glanced at my clothes. Almost automatically, I'd thrown on a white T-shirt, a black skirt and thick opaque tights, as I did most days. Ever since I began 'living as a woman', several years ago, my appearance, voice and persona had been dictated by external pressures: my expectation that the Gender Identity Clinic would decline hormone treatment if I didn't do enough to meet 'feminine' norms, and the experience of acquaintances or strangers mocking or abusing me if I did too much. The Gender Recognition Panel wanted me to declare exactly who I was, now and for the rest of my life. But I had to think harder – *was I the person I wanted to be?*

I decided to go out, in search of inspiration. Browsing through Twitter, something at the cinema caught my eye. 7pm: *Salomé* (1922). Bizarre silent version of Oscar Wilde's Biblical play.' I grabbed my bag and left, taking my seat just as the opening credits screened.

Nazimova

in

'SALOMÉ'

An Historical Phantasy

by

OSCAR WILDE

Intrigued by the nerve of this 'Nazimova' – who put her name above Wilde's! – I was hooked by the assertion that 'Salomé yet remains an uncontaminated blossom in a wilderness of evil' where King Herod had murdered her father, usurped the throne and married her mother. What would such an 'uncontaminated blossom' look like?

Then came Nazimova's answer. She bursts onto the screen in a glittering tunic and short skirt, crowned in a headpiece covered in pearls on springs, utterly imperious despite her miniscule frame. "You must not look at her!" commands an inter-title as she moves her plimsolled feet in tiny steps, holding her head above the gazes of Herod's courtiers, her dark lips pursed into an irresistible pout.

Like everyone else, I couldn't stop looking at her. She was utterly captivating – just as well, as nothing much was *happening*. What little action there was centred around Salomé's interminable attempt to seduce John the Baptist, imprisoned beneath the court (and called Jokanaan for some reason). After Jokanaan spurns Salomé's chess-like moves to 'kiss thy mouth', Herod, who's spent the whole film lusting over her with his tongue hanging out, tells Salomé that she can have whatever she desires if she will only dance for him. Salomé takes some persuading – she's not the kind of girl who'll jig whenever her stepfather claps – but sensing her chance for revenge, she acquiesces.

The inter-title promises 'The Dance of the Seven Veils'. But *where are the veils?* Surrounded by courtiers, yet *completely unveiled*, Nazimova tiptoes elegantly in a small, tight white dress; her hair is covered by a shocking bob wig, her frenzied eyes emboldened by heavy shadow and streaks of eyeliner. Finally, the courtiers find a veil, and when she throws her body to the ground, they throw it over her. She dances herself into a knot before untangling herself, rising and holding her single veil behind her head.

The dance complete, Salomé's demand is unflinching: "Give me the head of Jokanaan!"

Desperate not to kill his political prisoner, Herod offers *anything* else – a head-dress of peacock feathers, a frock fashioned from diamonds – but she stands firm. Finally, she gets her wish. She kisses Jokanaan's mouth, on his severed head, and cries "Love hath a bitter taste! But what matter? What matter?" What matter indeed – Herod screams "KILL THAT WOMAN!" and the courtiers descend and spear the impetuous princess to death.

★

Immediately, I wanted to see more of Nazimova. Only one other film, *Camille*, survives: the style was similar to *Salomé*, but despite the presence of Rudolph Valentino (at least until she had him cut from her death scene), it was nowhere near as captivating. Contemplating the sad loss of her work to history, I knew exactly who I wanted to be.

In many ways, her life differed from mine. Alla Nazimova was born Miriam Edez Adelaida Leventon in Yalta, Crimea to Russian parents and trained under Stanislavski at the Moscow Art Theatre, where she adopted her stage name. I'd been in Miss Lambert's form at a sixth form college in Horsham, where I got A-Levels in Theatre Studies and Performing Arts. She lived in a mansion on Sunset Boulevard, building the Garden of Allah, where she threw decadent parties for Hollywood's elite. I lived in a studio flat in Brighton, where I often ate Co-op tomato soup out of a tin. She had lesbian affairs with Surrealist artists, film directors, Oscar Wilde's niece Dolly, and Valentino's lover Natacha Rambova, who designed the costumes for 'Salomé', and possibly an affair with her *Camille* co-star himself. I'd not had so much as a message on OK Cupid for months.

Clearly, there would be limitations. For one, Madame, as she preferred to be called, was 5'3" and impossibly thin – but she hadn't let being 43 years old stop her playing the teenaged Salomé, so I figured it wouldn't dishonour her that I was a little bigger. (I'd aim to be to scale, at least.)

Another problem: not only were Rambova's fashions wildly impractical, but they had cost $350,000 – in 1922. But I wanted to become Nazimova, not Salomé. This, at least, freed me of the need to find a dress made of diamonds, but looking at the images online, I knew I'd still have to spend serious money on clothes.

I scoured Brighton's vintage stores for relics of the Twenties. I found a surprisingly large number that would have suited Madame, but not so many to fit me. Travelling to London, I fought through the retro shops on Brick Lane, telling myself that unlike the hipsters of Shoreditch and Dalston, I was an *artist*. I explained my project to a student who looked like an original Blitz Kid, and she grudgingly let me buy the glittering tunic that she'd found in the sale rail. I jostled my way to a svelte brown dress that resembled one I'd seen Madame wearing, a white mini-dress and a few other things that looked plausible and bought them, trying not to consider the gulf between her budget and mine.

I took a picture into a salon in Brighton and got an appointment.

"Who's that?" asked the hairdresser, "Lady Gaga?"

"Madame Nazimova," I replied, handing the photograph to her. "She was an actress."

"Oh right. What was she in?"

"'*Salomé.*'"

"Never heard of it," she said as she tried to force my hair into Madame's vivacious bouffant.

"Do you want me to colour it?" she asked, looking at the black and white photograph.

"Do what you can."

"Okay hon, pop your head forward," she told me, and started cutting.

An hour and £70 later, I realised I'd have to buy some wigs. That was okay – Madame wore them a lot – and on the plus side, I could replicate her headpiece using beads instead of pearls. So after spending an afternoon traipsing around the North Lanes to find a brown bouffant and a white bob, and an evening trying to put beads on springs and then attach them to a headband, my first outfit was complete.

I stared at the mirror, eyeing myself in the wig, tiara, tunic, skirt and little white plimsolls, practising Madame's *almost* inimitable pout. I copied her make-up from the film – pale foundation, two coats of black mascara, lashings of eyeliner and the darkest red lipstick I could find. But Madame wouldn't get so dolled up for a quiet night in, would she? (At least, not alone). I checked the listings to see what was on. One thing leapt out:

Masquerade
Celebrity Night @ Marilyn's
Featuring PENNY FARTHING, CANDY
STYXX and MC MARIA MAXWELL
Entry £5 — or FREE if you're FAMOUS!

Perfect! I called a few friends and asked if they fancied it. "You? Going to Marilyn's?" they scoffed. I told them I had a new outfit (which was true) and wanted somewhere to show it off (also true). This swayed them, so we agreed to meet there. I took my favourite handbag – the only one that I thought Madame might have been seen with – and threw in my make-up, phone and purse, and my favourite picture of Nazimova. I was ready to go.

But how to get there? I had no change for the bus, and it was a forty-minute walk to St James's Street, through central Brighton and past the seafront on a busy Saturday night. I bet Madame never had to walk anywhere: she'd have been chauffeured in the finest automobiles, I imagined, or ushered around in a gold-plated carriage by some nubile young men. She certainly wouldn't have had to get the Number 7 full of day-tripping drunks.

I set off for the nearest cashpoint, concentrating on replicating Madame's delicate footsteps. So I wasn't ready for the people who drove past, laughed "Tranny!" and threw a beer can at my head (missing) as they sped off. Undeterred, I continued. I could see a big crowd outside the church, perhaps leaving a wedding, the men in starched suits and the women in flowing dresses. *They must not look at me,* I thought, knowing that they would. I stood tall, pursing my lips to show that I was above their stares. Someone with a pram eyeballed me as she moved her child out of the way, even though I took measured steps around her, and a group of elderly ladies talked about me, glancing conspiratorially like the courtiers did at Salomé.

Ignoring wolf whistles from the bus stop, I could see the cashpoint across Seven Dials. There were three lads stood next to it, outside the off license. There was nowhere else to get money, so I watched from across the road, hoping they'd leave. It started to rain. I had no umbrella (can you *imagine* Madame with such a thing?) and it would ruin my make-up. So I rushed over the roundabout and darted towards the cashpoint, bank card in hand as an angry motorist swerved and swore at me. Withdrawing my money, I heard a voice: "That's a *man!*" Knowing where this may lead, I gestured at the machine, urging haste. "Bender!"

Laughter. The notes came. I stuffed them into my bag. I turned. They blocked my path.

What would Madame do?

I stood on tiptoes and kissed the biggest man on the lips. I walked on, head high, then started running as fast as I could without ruining my outfit as they chased after me. I skipped past some startled shoppers, shoved a sandwich board for a Thai restaurant in front of my attackers and, as they stumbled, hailed a passing taxi. "To Marilyn's!" I commanded as I threw myself onto the seat, locking the door as it raced through the changing light, smiling as I saw my man wipe my lipstick off his face.

★

I stepped out of the cab, dreaming of being mobbed by adoring fans. As it turned out, Steph, Orla and Madeleine were huddled outside smoking, trying not to get wet.

"You didn't come as celebrities!"

"Nor did you," said Orla.

"This isn't how I usually dress, is it?" I replied, hands on hips.

"We wouldn't come near you if it was, sweetheart. Come on, we're getting soaked," said Orla, beckoning us all inside.

I realised that I'd spoken without ever hearing a word from Madame. Apparently, she had a fine voice, theatrically trained, but her accent – a strange mixture of Russian, German and French – had destroyed her career on the arrival of the 'talkies'. I'd had some speech therapy on the NHS, but I suspect I didn't sound like a leading light of the Moscow Art Theatre. And how would she have competed with the Scissor Sisters at maximum volume? *She may have preferred to remain silent, and that the pictures had too,* I thought as the drag queen on the door stopped me.

"Five pounds please, darling."

"I don't think so."

"Don't you recognise her?" said Steph. "From Sunset Boulevard?"

"You're Gloria Swanson?"

"No, I am *not.*"

"Who the fuck are you then, darling? Eartha Kitt?"

"I am *Madame Nazimova*," I insisted, showing her the picture.

"Gorgeous," she replied. "Five pounds, please."

Angrily, I handed over the money and stormed upstairs, my friends giggling behind me.

We stood at the bar, celeb-spotting and gender-guessing. Amy Winehouse was a man, we were sure; Ryan Gosling definitely *wasn't*. Male and female David Bowies jostled for drinks whilst someone brave enough to attempt Gaga's meat dress fumbled anxiously at a steak, stinking out the sweaty room until the barman told her to get changed or get out.

I got a vodka and tonic (I didn't know Madame's favourite tipple) and we watched the cabaret. They were inviting people to perform: after a Madonna in a pink dress and faux diamonds butchered 'Material Girl', we laughed as the 'Vogue', 'Erotic' and 'Music'-era Madonnas booed her off and the drag queen compere took the microphone.

"Right, which 'Britain's Got Talent' reject is next?"

Steph shoved me towards the front. "Pick her! She'd die to be on stage!"

"Oh my Lord! Who on earth are you?"

"She's Madame *Nazimova*!" laughed Madeleine. "Get her on!"

"Madam Nazi-what? What's your act, love? Goose-stepping?"

"I perform the Dance of the Seven Veils… but not here," I said, trying in vain to back away from the stage.

"I think we all want to see the Dance of the Seven Veils, don't we?"

A huge cheer went up. Steph, Madeleine and Orla clapped and chanted "Dance! Dance! Dance!" and before I knew it, the clubbers were as transfixed as Herod's courtiers. A wave of hands forced me on stage to applause and whistles. Then, just as a grave realisation hit me, the compere piped up –

"Where are your bloody *veils*, Madam?"

If only to shut her up, I danced without them. I stood, arms above my head, then leant back, tiptoeing in a circle to absolute silence. I could see the crowd starting to talk about me, perhaps discussing my lack of classical ballet training as I quickened my pace, whirling frantically as they clapped ever faster.

"She *is* goose-stepping!" yelled the compere. "Can we get her at least *one* fucking veil? Preferably over her face?"

I saw movement at the bar, then a white sheet being passed towards the stage. The compere grabbed it and threw it over my head, saying "Got any more?" I twirled maniacally, ensnared in the heavy fabric, until I fell to my knees, exhausted. Hearing bemused murmurs from the crowd, I threw it off as I leapt to my feet.

"What the fuck was *that*, sweetheart? Go on, 'Madam' – piss off!"

I took a bow and stepped down, my reception as muted as that given to Salomé all those years ago. As 'Man, I Feel Like a Woman' kicked in, and I reflected that perhaps the world *still* wasn't ready for Nazimova, a handsome stranger with slicked-back hair took my hand.

"Please tell me you're Valentino."

"I wish!" he said. "I'm John. I didn't dress up. I liked your dance."

"I'm glad someone did."

"May I buy you a drink, *Madame*?"

Madame may have preferred a woman, I thought, and in truth so would I, but I felt sure she'd have gone with someone this suave. He took me to the bar, and I told him everything I knew about Nazimova, and explained why I wanted to call him Jokanaan. I assured him that I wouldn't demand his head on a plate – as long as he let me kiss his mouth. He did: we talked the night away, and when closing time came, we took a taxi back to his flat. It wasn't Sunset Boulevard, but I didn't care.

★

I woke in Jokanaan's bed, the white bob and head-dress thrown atop my tunic and plimsolls. I could hear driving rain against his window, and I sensed that the temperature had dropped sharply. I went to the bathroom and removed my smudged make-up, wincing at the sight of my sweaty fringe strewn across my forehead. I asked my man if he had anything I could wear home. He rummaged through his wardrobe, throwing a white T-shirt over my head before digging out an old jumper, denim jeans and some trainers that he thought might fit me.

Promising to return them soon, I trudged home, resolving never again to feel as grey as I did in his faded clothes. Picking up the Gender Recognition Certificate, I thought that with a bit more planning, I might be able to sustain this persona. After all, if the money ran out, that would only make me more authentic. Finally, I completed the form:

Statutory Declaration
Gender Recognition Act 2004

"I Alla Nazimova do solemnly and sincerely declare that:
1. I am over 18 years of age.
2. I have lived as a male / female (delete word that does not apply) throughout the period of _____ years since I transitioned in _____ (month and year of transition).
3. I intend to live as a Nazimova (delete word that does not apply) until death.

THE WOMAN IN
THE PORTRAIT

'Self-Portrait with Model (Selbstbildnis mit Modell)' remains the best-known work by German artist Christian Schad, nicknamed 'the painter with the scalpel' for the cutting, forensic nature of his work. The son of a wealthy Bavarian lawyer who supported him for half his life, Schad was born in Miesbach, Germany in 1894 and fled to Switzerland in 1915 to avoid military service. There, he became involved with the Dadaists, attending their legendary Cabaret Voltaire in Zürich, before moving to Naples and adopting the *Neue Sachlichkeit* (New Objectivity) style that replaced Expressionism as Germany's dominant Modernist form in the mid-1920s.

Painted in 1927 and currently on display at the Tate Modern, where it is on loan from a private collector, 'Self-Portrait' is noted for its mood of suspicion and hostility, and the disconnection between the artist and his 'model', whose identity has long been a mystery. It is not Schad's then-wife, Marcella Arcangeli, an Italian medical professor's daughter whom he married in 1923. Schad claimed that he saw the model in a stationery shop in Vienna, where he lived from 1925 to 1927, but the remarkable find of two diaries from 1926 and 1927, by a 'transvestite' known only as Heike, a hostess at Berlin's Eldorado nightclub who worked as a maid at Magnus Hirschfeld's Institute of Sexual Science, has radically changed perceptions of Schad's work. They were donated to Berlin's Schwules (LGBT) Museum by an anonymous man in Nice, near Hirschfeld's home after his exile from Germany, who realised their importance after years of them being kept as a family heirloom. Along with Schad's letters to Dadaist friends, recently discovered by art scholars, they explain how Heike came to be the woman in the portrait, and provide a fascinating insight into gender-variant life in the Weimar Republic.

★

On Friday 4 February 1927, Heike went to the Eldorado, a gay club in Berlin which had just moved to Schöneberg, opposite the Scala Variety Theatre. The following day, she wrote:

At the Eldorado last night, with Dora and the girls. I got my hair done like Asta Nielsen in Joyless Street, *and I wore my long black dress with the beads that Marie got for my birthday. Conrad [Veidt] was there, getting drunk with Marlene [Dietrich] before her act.*

I went on stage and introduced Marlene. A man at the front kept staring at me. I saw him go to the bar and buy some chips for a dance. As I stepped down, he grabbed my hands, told me that he'd just moved to Berlin, took me to the bar and bought a bottle of absinthe. 'You're the most beautiful woman I've ever seen,' he told me. 'Listen,' I said, 'I'm the third sex.'

'That might be Dr Hirschfeld's line,' he yelled, 'but you transcend *sex!' He invited me to his studio in Vienna to model for him. I said I wanted to be in the movies but Conrad told me it could never happen.*

'Ignore that two-bit somnambulist! Once they see my portrait, no director could resist you! As far as the pictures are concerned — you are a woman!'

We danced. He kept staring into my eyes, smiling. I tried to kiss him. 'I'm married,' he said. He gave me a card with his address, told me to write to him, and then left. Dora asked what happened. 'Nothing,' I told her.

★

After work on Friday 25 February, Heike arranged to meet Schad. She thought they would go for dinner and then to the theatre, and her diaries detailed her dreams of leaving her domestic service to become an actress, but Schad's note to Richard Huelsenbeck, posted earlier that week, suggests that he never intended to meet her in public.

Welt-Dada,

Went to Eldorado to find The Model — HEIKE. She — he — is Uranian — an invert — but thinks I'll make her the new Pola Negri — will take her to a hotel — see what transpires.

★

Heike's diary for Tuesday 1 March gives her side of their encounter in Berlin's Hotel Adlon.

I got to the Adlon at 5pm. 'From Morning to Midnight' by Georg Kaiser was on at the Neues Schauspielhaus, and I asked if we could go. 'I need the time to paint you,' said Christian. I saw that his easel was already set up. He drew the curtains. 'Take off your clothes and lie on the bed,' he told me. 'Would anyone cast me if I was famous for being naked?' I asked.

'How do you think Garbo got on Joyless Street*?' he replied, laughing. 'Take off your clothes and lie down.' He glared at me as*

21

I removed my hat. He stared at my hairline, then caught my eyes. I turned around and took off my blouse, and then my shoes and skirt, and started to pull down my stockings. 'Keep them on', he said. I turned back to him. 'Just the stockings.' I took off my bra and the inserts, and he just stared at me as I put them on the floor. Then I removed my drawers and lay on the bed.

He looked at my genitalia. I thought he was going to be one of those men who vomit, but he just stood there, breathing heavily. 'I thought you said we transcend sex.' Silence. 'The Doctor says we're more beautiful than other women, because we have to –' He pushed me on to the bed. 'Enough about Hirschfeld!' He kissed me – I let him. He was so coarse and so rough – he just wouldn't stop. Finally, he got tired.

'I know what you're thinking,' he said, looking at my sex again. 'I can't.'

'Why not?'

'They'll send me to prison!' He looked into my eyes. 'I'm not an invert!'

'No, you're not,' I said. 'I'm a woman, and as soon as the doctors get there with Dora, I'll be complete.'

He laughed. 'You're all the same, aren't you? Your special doctors – you just let them own you!'

I stroked his hand. 'Are you jealous of them?' I said.

He turned me over and screwed me harder than I'd ever been screwed. I screamed. 'Be quiet,' he whispered, 'someone might hear.' Then he stopped and shoved my face into the pillow. I sat up and looked at him.

He slapped me hard on the cheek, and then sat with his back to me. 'My wife... my son...'

I stared at the wall.

'I'm sorry,' he said.

'I'll talk to Conrad and Marlene,' I replied. 'They'll introduce me to Pabst and Lang. I'll start with bit parts but they'll see, and once they do, I'll pay for your art, I'll –'

'Shut up, you idiot!' he said. 'They might make films about freaks but they don't cast them!'

'I thought you liked freaks,' I said, reminding him that Marie had seen him at the Onkel Pelle.

'Not when they seduce me!' he yelled. He stood over me.

'Should I leave?' I asked. He nodded. 'I'll go,' I said, 'just don't hit me again.' He didn't move. 'I'll put on my clothes, just let me out!'

Silence.

'What about the portrait?' I asked.

'I can do it from memory,' he said.

He went and stood by the window. I got dressed and went to the door. 'Goodbye, then.' He looked at me and then turned his back. I heard him open the curtains as I left.

Soon after, Schad painted his 'Self-Portrait'. It was premiered in a solo exhibition at the Galerie Neumann-Nierendorf in Berlin, although we know that Heike was not invited. Schad sent her a letter, dated Monday 3 October 1927, quoted in Heike's diary two days later.

Heike,
The exhibition opened tonight – sorry you weren't there, and about the Adlon, but nobody can know that you were the woman in the portrait – I hope you understand. Marcella and I are finished and I am moving back to Berlin – perhaps I will see you at the Eldorado.
Christian.

★

'Self-Portrait' immediately caught the attention of critics, who cited it as one of Schad's most arresting works. Influential journalist and psychologist Rudolf Arnheim drew a comparison with another of Schad's works, which has assumed a new dimension since the discovery of Heike's diaries.

''Self-Portrait with Model' is outstanding, with Christian Schad including himself among the dilettantes, bohemians, degenerates and freaks who populate his world. With the decadent city as a backdrop, Schad is in the foreground, wearing just a transparent shirt which serves only to highlight his nakedness. The artist stares outwards, as if the viewer has personally intruded on Schad's clandestine moment of intimacy, his face filled with revulsion, heightened by the narcissus that points towards him, coming from the near-naked woman behind him. He blocks her midriff, perhaps protecting her modesty, or maybe hiding something from the intruder. Unwomanly despite her round breasts, she wears nothing but a black ribbon around her wrist and a red stocking, looking away from the artist, stunned if not scared. They both look alone: there are just a few inches between them, yet the distance is huge, and it is impossible not to wonder if Schad's self-disgust and the scar on her cheek are connected.

The 'model' is unnamed, but she bears a striking resemblance to the transvestite in Schad's 'Count St. Genois d'Anneaucourt', which depicts a disgraced Austro-Hungarian aristocrat caught between his public image and his desires, and between virtue and vice. The Count stands in the centre, ambivalent, seemingly hoping that the viewer will help solve his dilemma: Baroness Glaser, the demure, respectable woman to his right; or the tall invert, a performer at Berlin's Eldorado, to his left, his cheeks plastered in rouge, his huge frame barely covered by the transparent red dress that exposes his backside? Either way, the transvestite's resemblance to the 'woman' in the 'Self-Portrait' is noticeable, although Schad claims that the model was chosen through a chance encounter in Vienna.'

★

Heike saw 'Self-Portrait' later that week, recording her thoughts in the final entry of the recovered diaries.

Went to the Galerie Neumann-Nierendorf to see Christian's exhibition. I was alone – none of the girls could make it – and as soon as I got there, a group of society women stared at me, and then went back to the paintings. Of course they were fawning over the one of the dandies who wants to have sex with the hostess from the Eldorado but can't because it's not respectable. 'So brave!' they kept saying. 'So bold!'

I decided to find the picture of me, even though Dora told me not to. I should have listened to her. I'd tried not to expect anything but hoped he might have tried to bring out something of me – something to show Marlene or Conrad, or even the girls – but then I saw 'Self-Portrait with Model'.

I stared at it. Some woman glanced at me like I was dirt, looked back at the painting and then walked away. He'd made a very good likeness of himself, but he'd brought my hairline down and changed the style, made my nose bigger and given me breasts. He knew how much I wish mine were like that! Of course, he'd done that because he doesn't want anyone to find out how much he likes the third sex, and in the picture, he was blocking me from the waist down. He remembered my stocking though – he was so desperate for me to keep it on – and he added a flower. The gallery attendant said, 'It's a narcissus, it represents vanity.' Then I noticed the scar on my cheek – the attendant just shook his head when I asked what it meant. A man said they were common in southern Italy – jealous husbands put them on their wives. I could feel the tears coming. I ran back to the Institute and wept, and told Dora that I never want to see Christian or his painting again.

★

In summer 1932, Schad had another encounter with Heike in the Eldorado, which had moved to another location in Schöneberg, on Motzstraße – this was almost certainly their last. We know this from another letter to Huelsenbeck, dated Sunday 7 August.

Welt-Dada,
I promised myself I'd never go again, but last night I found myself in the Eldorado. It's been five years, but I'd only been there ten minutes when who comes on stage but Heike, from my Portrait. *She wore this glittering red dress, almost transparent, and I felt scared. As she got down, I called her. She recognised me and tried to run to the bar. I grabbed her wrist.*
   'I won't hurt you.'
   She looked at me, trembling. A couple of the inverts came over. 'I'm fine,' she said, and sat with me. I thought about when you said that being with her would be the perfect Dada gesture because she was so spectacularly ugly in the Portrait, *but I was stunned at how good she looked – just like when I first met her.*
   'You look incredible,' I told her. She thanked me. 'I can't believe that Marlene is in Hollywood and you're still here.'
   'You were right,' she said. 'They don't cast freaks.'
   Silence.
   'Did Dr Hirschfeld ...'
   'Dr Abraham got there with Dora,' she said. 'I'm fourth in line. Next year, they hope, if things calm down.'
   'Which things?'
   'Hitler says that Dr Hirschfeld is the most dangerous man in Germany,' she told me, 'and if he gets in ...'
   'My career is finished,' I said.
   'Your career and my life!' she shouted. 'The club, the surgery, the Institute, everything!' Silence. 'I might die on the operating table, anyway, like Lili.' She took a draw on a cigarette. 'That might not be so bad.'

'You don't need surgery,' I said, 'you're beautiful as it is.'

'If that's so, why did you cover me?' she asked. 'It wasn't a mistake – I could tell from that scar you put on my face.'

'I was breaking up with Marcella,' I told her. 'I didn't want to hurt her any more by letting her know I'd been with you.'

'The Count's shameful secret,' she said. 'Your shameful secret.'

'She's dead,' I said. 'Drowned. Last year.'

'I'm sorry,' she replied.

'There's no need to stay here,' I told her. 'Come away with me.'

'Where can I go?'

She started crying. I held her hand and I was sorry. She went back to her friends. I doubt I'll ever see her again. Will paint to work out how I feel about this. Let's talk soon.

Christian.

★

In October 1932, Franz von Papen, the right-wing Chancellor of the Republic, banned same-sex couples from dancing together in public after a long campaign against "the depraved night of Berlin", and in December, police chief Kurt Melcher ordered the closure of the "homosexual dance pleasures" in the city, killing the clubs where Heike worked. Hitler became Chancellor one month later, and as well as stepping up the attacks on Germany's LGBT population, the Nazis resolved to destroy its Modernist culture.

Schad was not targeted, having joined the National Socialist German Workers' Party (NSDAP) in 1933, and was allowed to submit to the Great German Exhibition of 1934. Many of his Dadaist associates and *Neue Sachlichkeit* contemporaries featured in the notorious Degenerate Art exhibition, but Schad was included in the Great German Art show, which the Nazis held as an antidote to the

Modern works they despised. Schad said he joined the Party merely to satisfy his 'bourgeois' father, and that he was 'kicked out' in 1942, but he remained in Germany during the war, moving to Aschaffenberg in 1943, after his studio was destroyed in a bombing raid. (A museum dedicated to Schad opened in the city in 2000 and holds evidence of him continuing to benefit from Nazi membership, receiving money and supplies, into 1943.) Schad remarried in 1947, five years after meeting young actress Bettina Mittelstädt when looking for a model; when he resumed painting in the 1950s, his style had become kitsch. He died in Stuttgart in February 1982, aged eighty-seven.

After Schad's letter, we know no more about Heike. Students raided Hirschfeld's Institute on 6 May 1933, and the Nazis seized its records and destroyed its library before repurposing the buildings to house the General Association of German Anti-Communist Organisations and the Institute of Studies relating to the Jewish Question. They made the Eldorado's final location on Motzstraße – to which Ernst Röhm had been a frequent visitor – into the SA's headquarters. Dora Richter had already tried to flee Germany but failed, and she was never seen again after the attack. We can only assume that Heike disappeared with her.

SURVEILLANCE CITY

Promising herself that she would not evade the flickering cursor for more than a few moments, Anne O'Hanlon could not resist Googling her own name. As ever, the first result was her Wikipedia entry:

> **Anne O'Hanlon** (born Leytonstone, London, 3 May 1979) is a British journalist who has featured in *The Guardian, The Times* and other publications. Since completing her PhD on second wave feminist organisations in London before and after Margaret Thatcher came to power, she has written extensively on the impact of the coalition's spending cuts on women, domestic violence, and online privacy, whilst her *Open Democracy* essay 'How London became Surveillance City' helped her to be short-listed for the Orwell Prize for political journalism.

She hated the photo: her hair was frizzy, and the way the light hit her nose made it look huge. She thought about deleting it, or adding further publications who had employed her, but then remembered that columnist who was caught editing his entry up and his enemies' down, killing his career, and went to check her Twitter notifications.

No new followers that morning – unlike her ex, whose new op-ed on 'the crisis of masculinity' was *everywhere* – so she returned to Google. For years, she'd been bored with *'Can you be a feminist and* [do X]*'* debates in activist circles and mainstream media, but the question of *Can you be a feminist and a masochist* had long bothered her. Only recently had she allowed herself to look up women writers who'd addressed it, getting no further than a few blog posts and opinion pieces.

She took a breath before typing 'BDSM community'. Several networks came up: she went for KinkNet, which invited her to join. Calling herself 'Kollontai79', she picked 'Female' as her gender and 'Heteroflexible' as her sexual orientation from a bewildering array of options, hesitating over her role before deciding on 'submissive'. She chose an image of two high-heeled feet walking downstairs from VALIE EXPORT's film '*Syntagma*' to illustrate her new profile, then looked up some groups. Trembling, she copied her About You section into a post in Submissive Women (London):

> I'm a 35-year-old woman, professional, slim with long brown hair, looking to explore her submissive side in private with a master or mistress.

She returned to her article, on how National Health Service cuts were affecting abortion clinics. A notification on her phone: 'Prince_Vibescu messaged you on KinkNet!'

> My partner (Belle_Captive) and I are intrigued. Please see our profiles but know that we are a couple who like to involve women like you, and that we have a well-equipped dungeon to explore your needs. If you're interested, write and send a photo.
> Alan and Catherine x

She checked his profile:

By day, I am a respectable public official. By night, I
will degrade and disgrace you. I like to be in control: if
you're an independent, intelligent woman, I will break
you with bondage, spanking, subjugation and humiliation. Over time, my partner and I will reach a place
where your imagination, memory and desires will
do most of our work. Then we can push you through
boundaries you didn't even know you had with a few
well-chosen words.

She replied:

I'm intrigued. Anne x

Then, immediately:

I'm PrinceVibescu on Skype. Call at 9pm tomorrow.
Wear a black low-cut top and red miniskirt, bare legs
and heels. We'll be waiting for you.

She cancelled her plans – dinner with an editor from
The Independent – and went into town. She didn't know
any sex shops, and thought the high street might prove less
embarrassing. Wrong: the assistant in New Look, probably
half her age, giggled when she asked about the miniskirt,
smirking at her colleague as she ran it through the till. She
left, silently, wondering if she *had* already started doing
Alan's work.

Back home, she breathed in, pulled on the top and skirt,
put on her stilettos and opened Skype. Then she called,
guessing that they would want her on webcam.

"Good evening, comrade," said Alan, his deep brown

eyes, pencil-thin beard and low hairline striking her from the darkened room, his arm around a woman with long blonde hair.

"Comrade?"

"We know Kollontai," said Catherine. "Communist, are you?"

"Well… I believe in equality."

"You won't by the time we're done with you," Catherine continued, laughing. "What's your favourite lipstick, Annie?"

"Christian Dior. Addict."

"Put some on and kiss the camera."

Anne applied it, shaking.

"Relax, love. Slowly, evenly. Good girl. You're beautiful." Alan laughed; Catherine smiled and kissed him. Anne watched herself on the bottom right of the screen, her eyes aflame. "You like seeing us do this?" Anne nodded. "Good. Pull down your top so we can see your chest. Then get your lipstick and write 'Slave' across it."

Anne took her make-up to her breasts.

"She's doing it!" whispered Alan.

"Capital letters!" replied Catherine. "She knows she's *ours.*"

"Hold them to the camera," Alan demanded. Anne leaned towards the screen. "That's it, hold them up." Then a woman's voice: *"Sit down!"* Stunned, Anne sat. "Look at yourself, you little tart!" She shuddered. Catherine laughed: "Did you enjoy that, darling?"

"Yes, mistress."

"We thought you would," said Alan. "Come and meet us, we'd love to teach you some more. Send us some of your fantasies and we'll give you our address."

★

Anne left Barons Court tube and found the house in Hammersmith. Catherine, wearing a black corset and long skirt, carrying a riding crop, stood her before Alan, sat in the lounge, dressed in a black mesh T-shirt and PVC trousers.

"Very secretarial," said Catherine, drawing the curtains. "Pretty, but not what we wanted." Anne watched Alan leave. "Clothes off." She stripped to her underwear. Catherine took off her bra and gave her a white blouse and black pleated skirt. "Put these on." Anne did, and Catherine brought Alan back to inspect her.

"Lovely," he said as he put a striped tie on her. "Usable."

"We enjoyed your email," Catherine told her. "We can make your dreams happen. The first is easy." Alan sat and Catherine put her across his lap. He lifted her skirt and spanked her, ordering her to thank him for every strike.

After ten "Thank you Sirs", Catherine blindfolded her and led her upstairs. She knew it was Alan strapping her into a chair, cuffing her arms and then locking her ankles into a slider bar. She heard a mouse click, then familiar voices: *Pull down your top so we can see your chest. Then get your lipstick and write 'Slave' across it …*

"You recorded me?"

"Just to tease you," said Catherine. "We'd like to take some photographs, if that's okay."

"No."

"You won't be recognisable," said Alan. "Blindfolded and gagged."

"Wouldn't you *like* to see yourself so vulnerable?" Catherine stroked her knee. "You trust us, don't you?" Anne sighed and nodded. "We knew you would," said Catherine, kissing and then gagging her.

She heard pictures being taken. She had to relent, she realised, finding to her surprise that her anxieties dissipated. Might they reward her? She felt her nipples being clamped.

She yelped, muffled, then heard Catherine's voice: "That's too much. Give her some pleasure."

Anne waited, relieved, as the clamps were removed, then felt something metallic, lubricated, inserted into her. Then she remembered her stated desire to relinquish control of her orgasms, and for the next twenty minutes, surrendered delightedly to her helplessness.

★

Again, Anne couldn't resist her ex's Twitter feed. As she browsed it, a notification appeared.

> **Countess of Reigate** @CountessReigate · 30s
> .@PrinceVibescu @OHanlon79 Isn't that Anne
> O'Hanlon? Nose and hair are a dead giveaway. Not so
> anti-surveillance now, eh?

Her eyes widened: she clicked 'View conversation' and Alan's tweet came up.

> **Prince Vibescu** @PrinceVibescu · 5m
> Naughty girl in detention! Next one will be much more
> punishing. Talk soon x

Beneath the text, a picture of her in the chair. There were already a couple of retweets and favourites. She texted Alan:

> Take that picture off Twitter NOW

> **Alan**: What?

Anne: I told you I didn't want photos – not only do you press me into it but then you put them on Twitter. Remove them immediately.

Alan: Fuck – I thought that was a text message! So sorry. Will delete right away.

Anne: Please do. I'll keep checking until it's gone.

Moments later, Anne saw that it had been removed. She hammered her name into the search engine and found another tweet:

Countess of Reigate @CountessReigate · 4m
Turns out Anne O'Hanlon is quite into surveillance – and violence – LOL #hypocrite

Two retweets already. She tried to call Alan: no answer. She stared at the image. There were no details on Mistress of Reigate's profile: no email or website, just a cartoon avatar. She would have to ask publicly, which would only make things worse. She texted Alan again.

Anne: @CountessReigate – someone you know? She's tweeting that picture. Make her stop?

Alan: Sorry I missed your call – in a meeting. I don't know her but I'll DM her saying not to use my pics without permission, and that it was posted in error.

Anne checked Twitter again: two more retweets, and one reply –'How can you tell with that blindfold? J' Shaking, she returned to her NHS article. No use: she refreshed the page again. Still there, but no more reactions.

Alan: She's promised to take it down. Got to go but will mail you later. Don't panic x

She tried to keep calm. *Perhaps people wouldn't recognise me,* she thought, *or just won't care? Maybe it would just disappear into the digital morass.* She refreshed again: *gone.* Another name search found nothing more, so she continued writing, smoking, tentatively, trying to distract herself until Alan got in touch.

★

'Prince_Vibescu messaged you on KinkNet!'

So sorry about the picture – we'll make sure that no-one reposts it. On Skype tonight if you need us. We hope you accept our apology – we'd love to make it up to you soon x

She opened Skype and contacted Alan.

"We're so glad you called," said Catherine. "We're sure you're angry…"

"Look… I have a profile. Not a huge one, but big enough for this to do me damage."

"How?" asked Alan.

"I write about violence against women, surveillance-"

"We know," said Catherine.

"*How* do you know?"

"We looked you up from that tweet and saw your Wiki page, then your work. You're good."

"You've undermined that."

"I don't think so," said Alan.

"What if people stop commissioning me?"

"Why would they?" asked Catherine. "They might ask you to write about it."

"Nobody would take me seriously again."

"They'd admire your honesty," Alan insisted. Anne sighed, angrily.

"Can I ask a question?" said Catherine. "You don't have to answer, but I think you should."

"Alright," replied Anne, trembling.

"Deep down, do you *want* to be outed?"

"Do you want to out me?"

"Does the thought turn you on?" Catherine laughed. "Looks to me like it does."

"You put that photo up on purpose, didn't you?"

"No, darling, it *was* an accident," Catherine told her. "But a happy one, I think you'll find. We need to meet. Will you visit?"

"Yes, I think we should."

"Great. We'll send some dates. And the photos – we think you'll enjoy them."

Annoyed, Anne closed the call.

★

Alan and Catherine, business-like in their matching suits, handed Anne a sheet of paper, which she recognised as the initial email she'd sent them.

"Read," ordered Alan.

You dress me up in a crop top and short skirt, put me on a chain and take me shopping. I'm not allowed to speak, except when spoken to, perhaps when you tell the assistants that you own me, and want to buy clothes (bras, undies, corsets, stockings, outfits) for me to please you. You would tell them what you wanted, and I would have to model things for your approval – in front of staff and customers if necessary.

"We can do this," said Alan, "tying it in with another fantasy of yours – being made to come in public."

"How?"

"We'll put this in you," Catherine told her, holding up an egg, "and take you to a restaurant for food and fun. Sound good?"

Anne paused. "Okay."

"We'll take a bus to the Westfield shopping centre," said Alan.

"No way. Too busy."

"Maybe it'd be better if we went to one of the shops in Soho," said Catherine. "What would you prefer, Annie?"

"I don't know."

"It shouldn't be too crowded this early," Alan said, handing Ann the white blouse and black skirt they'd dressed her in last time. "Put these on and kneel down."

"Why should I?"

"Because we'll take you to the bedroom when we get home. Now get down."

Anne changed and knelt, before Alan collared her. Catherine lifted her skirt and inserted the egg. They led her to their car, blindfolded her, sat her on the back seat and drove into town. She had no idea how much time had passed as the car stopped.

"Where am I?" she asked.

"No talking!" yelled a male voice.

"Darling, we're near the shop. Just a couple of streets away. If you're worried about anyone recognising you, we can keep the blindfold on. Would you prefer that?"

"No… I want to push myself."

"Good girl." Catherine kissed her and then removed it, getting her out of the car. Alan led her through the car park basement to the lift. Frantically, she glanced around: nobody there, thankfully. Then the lift came, containing a prim-looking couple with two small children.

Alan put her in the corner, facing the wall. *Thank God the English are so reserved,* she thought, *and such prudes.* "They think you're filth," laughed Alan as the family left in astonishment, leading her onto the street. Now, she regretted conceding the blindfold: they were on a packed Tottenham Court Road, tourists pointing and laughing, teenaged boys jeering. *Look confident,* she thought, holding herself up. "You're enjoying this, aren't you?" asked Catherine. Anne nodded, reluctantly. As Alan whispered "head *down*", the egg vibrated: she'd almost forgotten it, and she struggled to keep her balance in her 4" stilettos, her body convulsing with joy.

Alan dragged Anne down Charing Cross Road and onto Old Compton Street. Bracing herself for more humiliation, here it seemed that nobody was bothered, pointing momentarily, even waving and cheering – perhaps this happened all the time in Soho? It was a short walk to the shop: Alan made her ring the bell, then handed her chain to the shop assistant. Anne saw a Shoplifters Will Be Prosecuted sign and gazed up at the security camera as she entered, then looked at the DVDs, basques and corsets, PVC and leather dresses, dildos, vibrators and other paraphernalia on sale.

"I want a uniform for our maid," said Alan. "She's going to be doing lots of domestic service, so it needs to be practical."

"Yes sir," said the assistant, before turning to Anne. "Blue, black or pink?"

"She'll try them all and we'll choose," said Catherine.

"Great!" The assistant handed three dresses, all with white frills on the cuffs and high hemline, to Anne. "They all come with an apron and choker. Changing room's just there."

Anne tried the blue first.

"Goes with her eyes," said Catherine.

"I think the pink would be better," replied the assistant, smiling.

"Try that," ordered Alan, and Anne changed again. As she stepped out, another couple entered.

"Excuse me," asked Catherine, "our sub is trying uniforms, and we're not sure whether to go for blue or pink."

"Hold the blue against you," said the woman. "Pink. Definitely."

"She'll have the pink and black," declared Catherine. "Annie, change and then pay the lady."

Anne handed over her debit card. Catherine made her carry the paper bag and they left. Alan tugged her hard along Tottenham Court Road, making her stumble, and there were going into the car park as two women walked towards them.

"Oh my God, that's Anne O'Hanlon! I saw her on *Newsnight* last week talking about CCTV!"

"Quick – get your phone!"

Anne tried to cover her face, but too late: they'd caught her and walked off, laughing.

"Take me home *now,*" she told Alan.

"You sign up to a website, confess all your perversions to it, write them all down for us, beg us to carry out your fantasies, spent your own money on clothes to please us," he replied, reaching for his remote control, "and then get angry when a stranger takes a picture of you?"

"Don't you *dare* turn that thing on," she snarled.

"It'll be alright," said Catherine. "Come on."

They encountered no more people as she took her to the car, just security cameras: the thought of people watching her on those made her weep. Catherine sat with her, placing an arm round her shoulder and a hand on her knee, stroking her until her tears stopped.

★

"Can I use your computer?" asked Anne as they stepped into Alan and Catherine's home.

"Of course," said Catherine, bringing a laptop. Anne opened Twitter. Her name was trending. She clicked on it and read some of the tweets.

Stan the Man @StanWithThePlan · 30m
Extraordinary rumours about Anne O'Hanlon going around. Anyone got a pic? ;)

It was obvious: dozens if not hundreds of people were sharing pictures of her being led around central London.

"I don't know what to do," she told Catherine.

"Read the direct messages."

Anne opened them. The first was from her ex.

Incredibly brave. You know it's not my thing but I've got your back. Call me if you need x

The next was from an editor at a major newspaper. Catherine read it aloud.

Is that you in those photos? Do you want to write something about it?

"I think you should," Alan told her. "I'm going to dictate something, which you should tweet."

"Go on…" she replied as Catherine took her hand.

"Yes, that is me in the photos," said Alan, *"and I'm not ashamed. I consented to everything. Article coming soon."*

Anne typed his words into the empty box.

"You can do it, darling. Take the leap."

She took a deep breath and pressed Tweet.

"How do you feel?" asked Catherine.

"Relieved... I feel relieved."

"People *will* support you," Alan continued. "We'll make sure of it. And your article will be brilliant, I know it."

She looked at her Twitter notifications. There were several hundred new followers, numerous retweets and favourites of posts where she was mentioned, and for the first time since she began blogging, let alone writing for national newspapers, she felt free of the weight of her own carefully constructed image. A new tweet appeared:

Maria Robins @MariaRobins · 15s
Can't wait — brilliant and beautiful writer MT @OHanlon79 that is me in the photos and I'm not ashamed. I consented. Article coming soon.

"Darling, you see?" said Catherine. "It'll be fine. Now shut down the computer and come with us, you deserve a treat." Alan took her upstairs; Catherine closed the door, laid her on the bed and put her hand up her skirt. As Alan kissed her, she wondered if they were filming, and thought about pushing him away so she could ask. Then she realised that she no longer cared, giving herself over to the pleasures they'd promised, trying to suspend her anxieties about where she'd drawn the line between permission and violation.

THE HOLIDAY CAMP

Sam Lightfoot was several feet taller than Snappy the Alligator, and for that reason alone, he thought he shouldn't be there. He paused, squinting at the words YOU MUST BE SHORTER THAN ME TO RIDE, watching the rain drop down Snappy's strangely forced half-smile. The go-kart track closed hours ago and anyone smaller than Snappy was probably in bed, and the last time he might have enjoyed a place like this was when he was little enough to race.

He entered the main building through the arcade, a few coins in his pocket. He put 10p into the penny pusher, knowing that if he thumped the glass, he'd get more money. Knowing also that this would get him thrown out, he didn't, but he won enough to play a coin-op game. Most of them were about ten years old: *Bomb Jack*, *Paperboy*, *Arkanoid*, even *Pole Position*. A few lads crowded around *Sonic Blast Man*, calling their friend a "poof" for not hitting the punch pad hard enough to smash the asteroid hurtling towards Earth.

He walked past the air hockey tables to the foyer, wondering whether his parents would have gone to the Prince Albert pub or the Casablanca Showbar. He tried the pub, who did not bother checking him for ID, where two middle-aged newlyweds were mangling 'I Got You Babe' – a favourite of his mother's. He had long suspected that karaoke was the worst thing in the world and was pleased not to waste much time on proving it.

He went to the showbar, wondering how his parents were celebrating their final night at the camp. They were near the back with a bottle of wine and a near-empty pint of lager.

"Where's Jen?"

"She got bored," his mother replied.

"Don't blame her," said his father. "This is bloody embarrassing."

"You wanted to stay. You know I hate this kind of thing."

Sam looked at the stage. There was a drag queen in a tiara, a green dress with a skirt down to her black stilettos and a sash saying 'Helen Heigh-Water' in gold script. Her wig had blonde curls, her blue eyes had long lashes and her lipstick shined red, smudged across her face as she swigged Prosecco from the bottle.

Swaying, she finished 'Big Spender'. "Seriously you posh fuckers," she yelled, "give me some money, I'd down to my last forty Benson & Hedges. Nobody's going to tell the DSS if you chuck a fiver onto the stage!" Sam was one of the few people to laugh, as a bloke at the back of the room yelled, "How many men have been through Helen Heigh-Water?"

Sam couldn't help laughing, but Helen ignored him "What do you faggots want, hand jobs? You're not so tight that you can't part with a tenner, are you?" She drank more Prosecco and burped loudly, attracting more laughter as well as some boos and jeers. "We'll auction it. Five pounds for a hand job. Do I hear five pounds? No? Four fifty? Anyone?"

"I'll give you a fiver to fuck off home," yelled Sam's father. "This place has gone down the bloody pan – last year we got the Bootleg Beatles!"

"Bootleg Beatles, darling?" asked Helen, hitching up her skirt. "Wouldn't you prefer to stick your John in my Ringo?"

Sam's mother got up and walked out. His father downed his Stella and followed. "Yesterday, you're not half the man you used to be!" he yelled as he left, to cheers and applause.

"Oh, please say to me / You'll let me be your man / And please say to me / You'll let me suck your dick," yelled Helen, to enthusiastic laughter from Sam and boos from almost everyone else. "Ah, screw you all," said Helen, winking at Sam and then hiccupping, looking at the DJ booth. "Sweetheart, that's your bloody cue, can I have the music please?"

The bleeps and drum machine kicked in, and Helen began slurring her way through 'Tainted Love' by Soft Cell. *Sometimes I feel I've got to run away, I've got to get away …*

Sam had an erection. His boxer shorts were too small; it was so sharp and painful that he raced out. "Fucking hell, love, it wasn't that bad, was it?" came from the stage, where the chorus should have been. *Touch me baby, tainted love…* He leant on Snappy, taking deep breaths to calm himself, and then walked back to the chalet. His parents had gone to bed, so he tiptoed into his room. Jen wasn't there. He wondered why she'd come – wasn't she too old for this?

Jen's suitcase was open. Sam took off his T-shirt, his jeans, his socks and his itchy boxer shorts and stood naked, gazing at the pyjamas on his pillow. He took a pair of white knickers with a lace front and put them on. Instantly, his erection sprang back. Terrified of tearing the stitching, he tore them off. He tried a pair of pink briefs, and then pulled some black tights over them, too thin to mask his hairy legs. He grabbed a white bra, putting one strap over each arm and one sock in each cup. He couldn't fasten it and the socks fell out. "Shit," he said, worrying that he was making

45

too much noise. He dropped the bra and put on a dress, white with a red sash. It barely covered his crotch.

He took a hairband and put It over his brown, floppy curtains. The door opened. He took it off.

Too late. Jen entered and shrieked with laughter. "What the fuck?"

"Shush!" said Sam. "You'll wake up mum and dad!"

"What's so funny?"

Sam didn't recognise the voice. A guy in a 'No Fear' T-shirt, about 17, lanky, cropped hair, came in. "This is your brother?"

"Sam, this is Rich," said Jen. "He's my–"

The door to his parents' room opened.

"Quick – under the covers!" whispered Jen, hiding him.

"What's going on in there?"

"It's fine," said Jen. "I just woke up Sam, that's all."

The door closed. Jen prized the covers out of Sam's hands, seeing him curled up, shaking.

"It's okay, he's gone." She paused. "How long have you been doing this?"

"This is the first time, I swear."

Jen smiled. "If you don't do everything I say, I'll tell everyone in Leatherhead."

"And I'll tell them you've been with some guy who isn't your boyfriend."

"As if they'll believe anything *you* say," said Rich. "Gaylord."

"Leave him alone." Jen smiled again. "Do you like doing this?"

"No! I just–"

"I think you do," she said, tugging down his skirt and slyly brushing his leg. "Come on, let's go to the disco. Get that dress off and I'll sort out your bra." He did, and Jen put the bra over his torso, fastened it, rolled up the socks and put them back.

"You'll want cotton wool next time, love. Sit still and I'll do your make-up." Sam noticed Rich glaring at him as Jen put foundation and blusher on him, then did his eyes, giving them beige shadow and long black lashes. He put the dress on, and she put the hairband back, handing him a mirror.

"Feel sexy yet?"

"Yeah!"

"Great, let's go. Quietly! Wear these."

Jen handed Sam some black heels, half a size too small. He crammed his feet into them, and they left. Sam strutted across the square, looking around nervously, with Jen and Rich behind him, holding hands.

"Walks like a girl, doesn't she?" laughed Jen.

"Nice legs, too."

By the go-kart track, Sam saw the lads from the arcade, smoking. He heard whispers, laughs, and then a wolf whistle. As he got closer, they cheered. One of them blocked his path. Jen and Rich kept going, holding their ground, and the boy moved. Sam walked on, faster, pretending not to hear them yell *fucking queer*.

They went to Casablanca's, where 'Blame It on the Boogie' was playing. Jen screamed, grabbed Sam's hand and yanked him to the dance floor. "Come on!" she shouted as Sam glanced at the rhythm-less forty-something couples. Rich took Jen's face and kissed her: she held him off, but he pressed harder. She soon gave in, and they snuck off to a corner. Sam watched as Rich kept kissing Jen, every time she tried to get up, and although he couldn't make out what they were saying, he figured it must concern him as they kept looking at him. He started to walk over but Rich caught his eye, kissed Jen and climbed over her, so he stopped.

Having nothing else to do, Sam danced. He saw someone he thought he'd met: tall, blue eyes, jutting cheek-bones, cherry lips with cropped, bleached hair, wearing an earring, tight white T-shirt and perfectly straight denim jeans. The man went to the bar and then turned to him.

"Why did you run off?"

"Have we met?"

"My name is Matt, but I think you know me as Helen."

"You recognise me?"

"You're the first fit boy I've seen here for years," said Matt. "Did you dress up for me?" Sam blushed and laughed. "I'll take that as a yes. It makes a nice change from the bald old fuckers and frigid trollops who usually come here."

"Those were my parents," said Sam.

"Come here, I'll teach you to dance," laughed Matt, taking Sam's hands, "as you clearly don't know." He led, and Sam wobbled. "This is your first time in heels, isn't it?"

Sam nodded as 'Everlasting Love' hit its chorus.

"Are you alright?" asked Matt.

"People keep staring at me."

"Fuck 'em," said Matt. "Come back to the performers' chalet, there's no-one there."

Sam looked over at Rich, who was all over Jen. They didn't notice him. He took Matt's hand and they left. Matt opened the door. The sofa was covered in Helen's clothes: the dress and sash draped across it with the wig and tiara thrown over them. Heels and frocks were everywhere, interspersed with make-up and hairpieces.

"Sorry about the mess."

"I liked you better as Helen."

"You want to try it?" Sam smiled. "Come on," said Matt, taking off Sam's dress. "You shouldn't be wearing this Top Shop bollocks." Matt looked in Sam's bra. "Socks?"

"This is my first time."

"Let's make it special then. Here," said Matt, handing Sam a pair of flesh-coloured silicone breast forms, "I got these through the post."

"Where from?" asked Sam, squeezing one of them.

"Transformation. You know it?"

Sam nodded. He'd seen their adverts in the *Sunday People*, promising 'From He to She – Instantly!' but had never spoken to anyone about it.

"Shall I put them in then?" asked Sam. Matt grabbed them and fitted them into his bra, pulling up the cups when he was done.

"You want to wear the green one, don't you?"

Sam smiled. Matt unzipped it and gave it to him to step into. Then Matt did it up and put a hairnet over Sam's head, topping it with the curly blonde wig and the tiara. He sat Sam in front of a mirror. "Lashes first, darling," he said, gluing some fake ones onto Sam's eyelids. "And now... glitter!" He smeared it across Sam's face. "Divine!" He paused, stroking Sam's shoulders, smiling at his reflection. "I'd do your lips, but..." Matt picked Sam up and kissed him. They looked into each other's eyes as Matt rubbed Sam's thigh, brushing the silk dress against his tights. Matt worked his hand up to Sam's crotch, rubbing his knickers, and then led him into the bedroom.

"You use a condom?" asked Sam.

"Always," said Matt. "So many of my friends dropped dead." He paused. "Get 'em off then."

Sam took off his underwear and laid on his front. Matt threw Sam's shirt over his back and fucked him until they both collapsed onto the bed.

"You okay?"

"It hurts."

"In a nice way?"

"Yeah."

"You'd better go," said Matt. "I don't know how old you are, and if anyone finds out then I'm in big trouble."

"If we were straight, it'd be legal," said Sam.

Silence.

"I'm afraid I'm going to have to ask for my tits back."

Sam laughed. He took off the dress, wig and hairnet and jutted out his chest, letting Matt take the breast forms. Matt kissed him again, handed him Jen's dress and picked up the socks.

"If you roll them up, they're more convincing," said Matt, putting them back. "And walk with your heel first."

"Thanks," said Sam.

"Keep the lashes, they suit you."

★

Sam left. Where was his chalet? He wandered across a few courtyards, and then remembered that Jen had the keys. Perhaps she was in? He saw their block, and their ground-floor chalet. A light was on: he crept closer, cursing the noise that his shoes made on the concrete, quickly realising that he could quieten it by walking over the damp grass.

Someone was in the living room. Was it Jen or his parents? The curtains were closed. He walked past the cinema, seeing that *Ace Ventura: Pet Detective* had been on. The same lads were outside, smoking. They eyed up his legs but said nothing. *Perhaps they think I'm a girl?* Sam tried to keep his head up, going for the disco. It was closed. *That must have been Jen,* he thought, *mum and dad will be in bed by now...*

He decided to avoid the cinema, taking another route back. Seeing Snappy, he felt like he'd found a friend. Then he realised that people were following him. Panicking, he stumbled in his heels, balancing himself on Snappy's snout.

"Are you a girl or a boy?"

"What?" said Sam, backing away as three lads cornered him against the go-kart entrance. "Man or a woman? Are you a man or a woman?" they sang. Sam tried to barge through, but they blocked him.

"You're a fucking geezer, aren't you?"

"Leave me alone!"

"Grab his wig!" said one, as his friend yanked at Sam's hair.

"That's real, you dick!"

"Don't call my mate a dick, you bender!"

Sam tried to run. Someone grabbed him and shoved him backwards.

"Those aren't your real tits, are they?"

He folded his arms over his chest and stood against Snappy, shaking.

What would Helen do?

Sam took off his heels and smacked one of the lads around the face with them. He ducked under Snappy and raced across the go-kart track, vaulting over its ridges, lifting the skirt of Jen's dress so it didn't impede his movement, and then ran to the chalet, praying that he wouldn't slip on the wet grass in his tights.

"I'll kill you!" he heard. "Faggot!"

Sam reached the chalet, desperately hoping that the door was unlocked. It was. He got inside, slammed it shut and bolted it. Struggling not to vomit, he leant on the handle, gasping for air. One of the boys banged on the door. "Get out here! Poof!" He started crying, then felt a hand on his shoulder. It was Jen.

"Are you okay? What happened?"

"Make them stop," said Sam, falling into her arms. He glanced over her shoulder at Rich, sat at the table looking at the *Daily Mail* sports section.

"Rich," said Jen, "tell them to piss off, would you?"

Rich sighed and went to the window, opening it a fraction. "Look, he's not coming out so you might as well fuck off, understand?" He closed it again, glaring at the boys until they walked off. Sam made for the bedroom.

"Hold on!" said Jen. "Where have you been? We spent ages looking for you!"

"You disappeared!"

"You disappeared! Where did you go?"

"I was dancing with Helen."

"That rubbish drag queen?"

"She's not rubbish!"

"She?" laughed Jen. "Wait – you don't fancy her, do you? I mean him."

"Shut up!" whispered Sam. "I've got to go and get–"

The door to their parents' room opened. Sam's father walked out, looked at him and laughed.

"What are you doing dressed up like that?"

Sam hesitated.

"It's for a competition," said Jen.

"Which competition was that?"

"Umm… we bet Sam that he couldn't win the Miss Lovely Legs contest."

"Why the hell would you want to do that?"

Before Sam could answer, his mother walked into the living room. She shrieked. "Why are you wearing your sister's clothes?" She looked at Sam's father. "Are you just letting him do this?"

"He says it's for a competition," said his father.

"I didn't say that!"

They heard voices outside, giggling. Rich went to the window. "I thought I told you lot to fuck off!" The lads jeered. Sam's father walked over. "He means it – get out of here or I'll call the police!" They laughed, shouting "wanker" and "paedo" as they walked away.

"Did you win the competition then Samantha?" asked Sam's father as his mother glared at him. "Funny time to have it – in my day they were in the afternoon. And they didn't have blokes!"

"There wasn't a competition," said Sam.

"Were you copying that drag queen?" asked his mother.

"No… I just wanted to see what it felt like."

"And how does it feel?" asked Jen, before their parents could. She offered Sam a seat.

"It feels…" Sam looked at his parents, and then Jen. "It feels nice."

"Go and get changed," said Sam's father. "And don't let us see you dressed like that again."

★

Sam's parents went to their room. Sam went to his, closed the door and stared at himself in the mirror before taking off his clothes and trying to sleep. The next morning, after she returned from Rich's chalet, Jen gave Sam a pair of knickers. "Keep them until you can be more open," she told him. Sam put them on under his jeans as he packed to leave, wondering when that time might arrive. As his parents silently drove though the exit, he sat in the back seat of their car, knowing he would never forget that strange freedom he had found at the camp.

REFLECTIONS ON VILLAPLANE

My father and I had walked many times together into the Stade Olympique, but this was the first time that Racing Club had reached the final of the Coupe de France, held at our team's home ground in Colombes on the outskirts of Paris, and he held my hand as we approached to stop me running off into the huge, febrile crowd.

As we queued to get in, my father reached into his wallet and handed me a ticket:

FÉDÉRATION FRANÇAISE
DE FOOTBALL
FINALE
COUPE DE FRANCE

Racing Club de France –FC Sète
Stade olympique Yves-du-Manoir, Paris
Entrance 28 – Standing area
Dimanche 27 Avril 1930.

"The garage has done well so I thought I'd get something special for your birthday," he said. "Whatever happens, make sure you enjoy it, son."

"Thanks Papa!" I said, hugging him. He rubbed my hair as I showed the ticket to the man on the turnstile and pushed my way into the stand.

"Stay with me!" shouted my father, limping as the turnstile always aggravated his leg, wounded by a German bullet at Verdun. I kept racing towards the terrace, already nearly full, trying to get as near to the front as possible. My father stopped underneath the Peugeot billboard at the back of the tiny strip behind the goal.

"Let's go here."

"Oh, come on, Papa!" I replied, feeling like we were miles from the action with the running track separating us from the pitch.

"We can't get any closer, it's packed. Here," he said, giving me the match day programme he'd bought outside. "Tell me who's in the team."

"Tassin's in goal," I told him. "Anatol and Capelle are the full-backs."

"I should hope so too, given how much we paid for them. Who's up front?"

"Veinante and Lhottka."

"No Delfour?"

"No, Papa."

"I think he's injured. Shame. Is Villaplane playing?"

"Yes, he's the half-back."

"We need a big game from Alex today," said my father. "If he can get on top of Cazal then I think we'll do it. Look, they're coming out."

Alexandre Villaplane followed Racing Club captain Manuel Anatol onto the pitch, in their usual light blue and white hoops with black shorts, alongside Louis Cazal, who wore the deep green of FC Sète. We clapped and cheered with the 35,000 crowd, nearly all Racing fans in flat caps, and the noise was deafening as the teams lined up for the national anthem.

"Look at Alex!" said my father as Villaplane put his hand on his heart and sang '*La Marseillaise*'. "That man would die for us. For Paris and for France."

"It says here he's Algerian, like us," I replied, that he was born in Algiers on Christmas Day 1905.

"No, son, he's French. Like you and me." He pointed at the main stand. "Do you see those two men in the box?" I nodded. "That's President Doumergue," he told me, referring to the leader of the Third Republic. "And next to him is Jean-Bernard Lévy. Do you know who he is?" I shook my head. "He owns Racing Club."

"Is he rich?"

"He bought all those players," said my father, as the teams got ready to kick off. "He made sure he got Alex first. Clever, isn't he?"

I nodded, reading about how Lévy, a 32-year-old businessman, had bought our team the previous summer and vowed to make us the best in France. It also said that Villaplane had made his name at FC Sète before joining SC Nîmois in 1927 and establishing himself in the national team. Although he had only been at the Stade Olympique for one season, it already felt like he *was* Racing Club. Villaplane wasn't the tallest but his calmness on the ball and his huge strides when trying to win it from his opponents, as well as his powerful leap to head clear or set up chances, made him seem giant.

Against Sète, he was immense. Time and again, he cut the supply lines to their star striker, Ivan Bek of Yugoslavia, with crunching, perfectly timed tackles, and then played intricate balls through their defence to his France team-mate Émile Veinante, or ambitious passes to the left and right wings, the supporters clapping as each found their target.

After eighty minutes, the match was still scoreless, the fans growing tense, but we started singing Villaplane's name as he knocked Cazal off the ball. It soon fell to Ferenc Lhottka, who confidently beat Sète goalkeeper Charles Frondas – 1-0 to us!

"Yes!" I screamed as my father embraced me. The crowd surged down the terrace: my father kept his arms around me to protect me from the crush, making sure I shielded his injured leg. Racing's players ran back to the halfway line, high-fiving and hugging each other. Villaplane held out his hands, urging his team and fans to remain calm, and it died down a little, but with just a few minutes left, everyone sang about how we would win the Cup, and I joined in.

"Not just yet, lad," my father told me, ever the pessimist. With seconds to go, Villaplane scuffed a clearance and it fell to Louis Cazal: after a desperate passage of play, the ball came to Alexandre Friedmann, who equalised. The Racing Club fans went quiet as the band of Sète supporters who'd travelled from the south went wild behind the other goal. Soon, the final whistle went, and my father put his arm around me. "Don't worry," he said as the players prepared for extra-time. "We've been the best team. We'll still do this."

The Stade Olympique fell silent as Villaplane sat his men in a circle, pointing to each in turn. Although we couldn't hear his words, we could see their faces, even star players like Anatol and Veinante, listening intently to every word from their younger team-mate.

"What's he saying, Papa?"

"I don't know," he whispered. "He's probably telling them to keep working as a team rather than trying to win it on their own, and to look out for each other."

The referee blew his whistle and Lhottka kicked off again. Almost immediately, it became clear that Villaplane's team-mates were not all as fast or fit as he was, and Sète played around him: his half-back partner Paul Guézou couldn't keep up with Bek, and the Yugoslav put Sète into the lead after just four minutes of extra-time. "We can still win!" I yelled as my father's face dropped, but fifteen minutes later Bek scored again, bursting past Villaplane in the penalty area and rifling home from Durand's cross. As Tassin kicked the ball out of the net, Villaplane dropped to his knees and slammed the ground, before Anatol took his arm and helped him up.

The match ended, and Villaplane offered handshakes to his opponents and friendly arms around his comrades' shoulders. "Don't cry, son," my father told me. "We'll be back next season."

We walked slowly, wordlessly up the steps as President Doumergue and Jules Rimet, the head of the *Fédération Française de Football,* handed the trophy to Sète coach Sydney Regan, turning only to see Villaplane embrace Cazal.

★

LE MIROIR DES SPORTS
Lundi 14 Juillet 1930
FRANCE VICTORIOUS IN
FIRST WORLD CUP MATCH

The first football World Cup began yesterday in Montevideo. Playing in the opening match to honour the tournament's founder, Jules Rimet, who has been a tireless advocate of friendly competition between nations, France were triumphant, beating Mexico by four goals to one in front of a small crowd at the Estadio Pocitos. The goals came from Lucien Laurent, Marcel Langiller and André Maschinot (2), but France owed their win to their fearless captain, Alexandre Villaplane of Racing Club, whose hard running, precise passing and tough tackling helped *Les Bleus* to assert their superiority from the start.

The following season, my father and I returned to Colombes, full of pride after reading about our captain, even though his team had lost 1-0 to both Argentina and Chile and gone out in the group stage. Now, however, Villaplane's performances were less enthusiastic and less energetic, and Racing Club were beaten 2-1 by OGC Nice in the first round of the Coupe de France. "So be it," said my father, "I can't afford all those Cup games any more." People around me stopped singing Villaplane's name, and instead they murmured about him being seen drunk at bars, taking his pick of the women in casinos and throwing cash around at the racetracks – none of which, said my father, befitted an amateur or a gentleman. The Depression had taken hold in France, not least on my father's automobile business, and although I refused to believe the rumours and tried to defend Alex's performances, we still wondered: *where was he getting his money?*

★

One March afternoon in 1932, I was at my father's garage in Montmartre, cleaning the showpiece Bugatti Type 49 convertible. It was black with a red trim, and I was polishing the bonnet until I could see the whiteness of my teeth in it, as my father had asked me to. A small but striking man, his dark hair in a side-parting, entered in an immaculate suit. I recognised him instantly, and was so stunned that I knocked over the bucket of water by my feet.

"Are you... Alex Villaplane?"

Seeing him without that running track keeping us apart,

I was struck by how narrow his shoulders were, and how the light from the window shone just below his hairline, greased back with Brylcreem. Although I'd seen so many of his brave clearances at Colombes, I'd never realised until now just how big and bold that forehead was.

He picked up the bucket and my sponge, handing them back to me with a generous smile.

"I am indeed."

I was trying to think what to say to him as my father came out of the office.

"What an honour!" he said. "The captain himself!"

"Are you Racing Club fans?" asked Villaplane.

"We go to every game at Colombes."

"Good! If you were Red Star supporters, I'd take my business elsewhere." My father laughed at the reference to Racing's local rivals, and shook Villaplane's hand. I ran into the office, took the Cup final programme from the cabinet and thrust it at Villaplane.

"Would you like my autograph, young man?"

"I'm sure he would," my father replied. Seeing the cover, Villaplane sighed, his face lifting slightly when he read the description of his career.

"The first North African to play for France," he read. "You are Algerian too, yes?"

"We're French," I said.

"I was from Algeria originally, but my son was born in Paris," my father told me. "A lifelong Racing Club supporter."

Villaplane scrawled his signature across the line-ups and gave the programme back to me. It was barely legible, but I didn't care. He put his hand back on the Bugatti.

"I want to buy this car."

"No disrespect," replied my father, "but you're an amateur. How could you afford it?"

"I run a successful automobile business in Sète, where I grew up," said Villaplane, calmly, and deliberately, "and I want to set up in Paris. I heard good things about you from Racing's sponsors, so I wondered if you might like to go into business with me. We would have your showroom here and mine on the south coast under common management, sharing the profits.

If you're interested, I have some information on my company, including accounts for the last five years." He gave my father a file and a business card. "You don't have to decide straight away." He looked at me. "I can trust your Papa, can't I?" I nodded. "Great!" he said, returning to my father. "Here's a cheque for the car. I'll be back next week and then we can talk more."

Villaplane gave the cheque to my father, shook his hand and left. I looked again at the programme, clutching it to my chest when my father tried to take it.

"Will you do it, Papa?"

"I don't know," he replied. "You've heard all the stories at Colombes."

"But you always told me that people will say anything about Algerians. And anyway, you said he hasn't done anything wrong."

"I know, but I need to check everything with the bank."

Ten days later, Villaplane returned.

"Did you cash my cheque?" he asked.

"She's yours," said my father. "Show Monsieur Villaplane to his car, will you?"

I ran to the Bugatti and opened the door. Villaplane jumped inside.

"Perfect," he said, stepping into to the car. He smiled again, one corner of his mouth rising as his eyes narrowed, and fixed their gaze on me. Then, more relaxed, he looked at my father.

"Did you consider my proposal?"

"I discussed it with the bank," replied my father. "They said your finances look sound."

"Our showroom does well," said Villaplane, "and I am told that professionalism is close to being legalised. M. Lévy has assured me that when that happens, I will become the highest-paid player in France. Between that and the business, we'll be fine." My father smiled, and Villaplane shook his hand. "Visit my men in Sète. If you like them, then we are ready."

"I will," said my father. "But first I need to sort out the paperwork for the car." He looked at me. "You talk to our guest while I find it."

As my father went into the office, Villaplane grabbed the steering wheel, grinning again.

"What was it like playing in the World Cup?" I asked.

"Oh, incredible," he said, his eyes fully open for the first time. "We got this huge boat with stained-glass windows and paintings from the Côte d'Azur to Uruguay. The *Conte Verde,* it was called. The Romanians and the Belgians were there, and the Brazilians joined us later. A few referees, too, so we had a chance to pay them off." He smiled at me, and I laughed. "I'm only joking – we were cheated with that disallowed goal against Argentina, as I'm sure you know." I nodded. "Anyway, we had to keep fit – Delfour gave us exercises – but it was fun, like a holiday camp. Then I was chosen as captain. Can you imagine what it's like to captain your country?" I shook my head.

"Well, it's hard to explain," he said, "but the day I took the field against Mexico was the greatest of my life, and the feeling when it ended, and we'd won the first ever match..."

"Why don't you play for France any more?"

Villaplane got out of the car and put his hand on my shoulder, looking me in the eye. "Son, you'll know that people will say anything about us Algerians, right?" I nodded. "The

French players started spreading rumours about me, and the Fédération believed them. It's all political," he said. He fixed me a menacing stare, his mouth open slightly, jutting out his forehead. "I know people say things at Racing Club, too, but luckily Monsieur Lévy knows who's telling the truth. You do, too, don't you?"

"Yes, sir," I gulped.

"You're a good lad, I can see. Can you persuade your father to work with me?"

"I'll try."

"I'll introduce you to all of your heroes," he said. "Capelle, Delfour, Veinante – everyone. If we win our semi-final against Cannes, then you can meet the President. How does that sound?"

"Great!" I said.

"Great." He offered his hand, and I shook it.

My father returned, finally, with the papers.

"Thank you so much," said Villaplane. "See you next Saturday."

"Perfect," my father replied. "Enjoy your Bugatti!"

"I will!"

Villaplane drove the car out. His eyed narrowed and he shot me a smile as he went.

"Are you going to do it, Papa?"

"I'm not sure."

"Oh, come on. You're not going to believe all those lies about him, are you?"

"Well, his cheque cleared. You're right – I should go and visit."

The next weekend, my father returned from the south coast, telling me that he could not wait to go into business with such a gentleman. Soon they were partners, with my father running the Paris office and Villaplane, the overall owner, managing the branch in Sète.

Four weeks later, my father found the showroom locked, and the land sold. He called the Sète branch: neither that number nor his contact for Villaplane in Paris were in use. He went all the way to Sète, finding a padlocked building with the signs and fittings removed. Weeping, he explained to my mother and me, saying that an anonymous caller had told him not to go to the police, and that even if he did, they wouldn't care about an Arab Algerian being robbed by a French Algerian, especially not one as powerful as Villaplane.

"I'm so sorry, Papa. I knew from how he looked at me when he drove away that you shouldn't have done it. But I told you to because I got excited about meeting all the players. He told me the rumours weren't true, and I believed him. It's all my fault."

"No it's not," he said. "I don't know how I let myself be taken in. I'd heard more than enough."

He winced. "I survived a bullet in the leg, I can survive this."

★

After my mother left, my father found work at the Renault factory in Boulogne-Billancourt and we moved to a small flat in Montrouge, on the edge of Paris. My father told me that he could never watch Racing Club again, but I missed our trips to the Stade Olympique, and we agreed that I might go back once Villaplane was gone. Even though my father had told me not to, I went to the police, explaining how Villaplane had stolen his business: they assured me that however untouchable he seemed, they would take the charges and any threats against us very seriously. Then they looked at the contract: there was no mention of how money would be split if the business were sold, and no proof of whether the sale had been discussed, so there was nothing they could do.

Days later, the FFF announced that professionalism would be legalised. Sochaux's president, Jean-Pierre Peugeot, had admitted to paying his players years earlier, and Lévy was involved in its introduction, telling the fans that this meant Racing Club could finally become the strongest team in the country. But he did not make Villaplane his highest earner: the captain was immediately sold to Olympique d'Antibes, in *Division 1 Groupe B* of the new national league, for what I imagined to be a large fee and a huge wage.

Antibes spent heavily, but I was still surprised when they won their section and beat *Groupe A* winners SC Fives Lille 5-0 in the deciding game. It soon emerged that the match had been fixed. Stripped of the championship, Antibes blamed their manager, Valère, but after sacking him, they quietly released three players: Laurent Henric, Louis Cazal and Villaplane. He joined OGC Nice for the 1933-34 season, but neither my father nor I returned to Colombes for their 4-3 defeat to Racing Club – that summer, they were relegated, with Villaplane's lazy, unprofessional displays widely blamed after he was fined for repeatedly missing training.

Then he spent three months with Hispano-Bastidienne de Bordeaux in the second division, rarely turning up and being fired. The next I heard of him was in 1935, when he was sent to prison for six months for fixing horse races in Paris and the Côte d'Azur. "If I'd have known," said my father, "I'd have testified against him." I suggested he go to the police now, but Alex was likely bankrupt, he said, and I could tell he never expected retribution for his loss.

On 5 May 1940, I went to Colombes, alone, and saw Racing Club beat Marseille 2-1 in the final of the Coupe de France. Five days later, the German invasion of Paris began. President Lévy, who had spoken out against the 1936 Olympics in Berlin and the FFF's refusal to allow anti-Mussolini demonstrations at France's 1938 World Cup quarter-final against Italy, played at the Stade Olympique, was killed during the first week.

My father and I both knew that as Arabic Algerians, we could be marked men. He insisted on staying in Paris, believing that his job would be safe, but he said I should leave, and I went to work as a typist in Bordeaux, There, I joined the Resistance, distributing handbills on arrests, acts of sabotage, and planned raids by *la Carlingue, known informally as* the French Gestapo.

Months later, one of those bills brought news of my father. At 3am on Saturday 7 September, the police had broken into our home and arrested him on trumped-up fraud charges. They delivered him to the *Carlingue*, who tortured and killed him. Then I heard: Villaplane had been released from prison, where he had been sent for handling stolen goods, and then he joined the gang.

*

The following year, after the Allied landings in North Africa, the German occupation spread across the country. I moved from Bordeaux to Mussidan, a village in the Dordogne in south-west France, working on a farm and gathering intelligence for the Resistance. On 11 June 1944, a BMW 328 rolled into the square. The *maquisards* (as the rural Resistance were known) had attacked an armoured train at the station that morning, and the Gestapo must have come for revenge. As I wondered how best to warn my comrades, the villagers opened their doors.

The car stopped, and a man stepped out. The first thing I noticed was the Nazi armbands. Then the narrow shoulders, and a cap that did not mask that huge forehead, which reflected the light of the afternoon sun: Alexandre Villaplane.

"Oh, what times we live in!" he told a priest, in that same measured, rehearsed tone that I'd heard at the garage. "Oh Father, this is a terrible age! To think that I, a proud Frenchman, am reduced to wearing a German uniform!" A crowd had assembled. "Have you seen, ladies, what atrocities these butchers have committed? They are going to kill you." He approached a silver-haired woman, in her late fifties, and placed his hand on her shoulder. "But I will try to save you, even as I risk my own life. I have already saved many people. Fifty-four, to be precise. You will be the fifty-fifth. If you give me 400,000 francs."

I watched, horrified, as she let Villaplane into her home, followed by three other men. I took aim, putting my finger on the trigger of my pistol. Then I remembered the Communist Party order not to assassinate individuals, and as the door closed, I ran to find my friends. It was too late: they had been arrested by the *Brigade Nord-Africaine*. An Arabic soldier pointed a gun at me, telling me to give up any weapons and join the others. My comrades and I were marched to a ditch and ordered to line up with our hands on our heads. I stood on the far right as three men in SS uniform marched into view.

Villaplane walked up to us, smiling.

"These are the criminals, captain," said one of his men.

"You shall dig your own graves," Villaplane told us, "unless you have 400,000 francs."

Nobody in this tiny village seemed to recognise him. Perhaps, like most people in France, they were more interested in cycling than football.

"Alex!" I said. He stopped, open-mouthed, narrow-eyed, staring at me. "You don't know me, but I watched you in Colombes."

"Drop your weapon," Villaplane told his soldier. "Keep the others here." He placed his arm around my shoulder. "Come with me," he said, leading me away.

I heard a voice from a comrade.

"You haven't got 400,000 francs, have you?"

"Shut up!" I shouted back. The BNA solider rammed a gun into my comrade's back as everyone else tried to stay still.

"No talking!" yelled Villaplane. Satisfied that order had been restored, he took me to a nearby farmhouse and sat me at the kitchen table.

"You are a Racing Club supporter?" he asked.

"My father and I went every week. We were so proud when you captained France."

He sighed. "That was the happiest day of my life."

"And now you wear a German uniform."

"I do it for France," he said. "To save as many French people as I can."

"For a price."

"What?"

"I saw you, telling people you'd help them. For 400,000 francs."

"Every centime goes towards my countrymen. For them, I even stole from the Germans. They caught me and I had to leave Paris. My friend Cazal sent me papers so I could go back."

"Louis Cazal? From Antibes?"

"Yes," said Villaplane. "We played together at Sète."

"And then you fixed the games together."

"I took a huge pay cut to join Antibes. What else was I supposed to do?" He lit a cigar. "Besides, everyone was doing it. They only checked us because nobody expected us to win."

"Wait," I said. "Pay cut?"

"You didn't believe that we were amateurs, did you?" He paused. "You probably thought that *you* were funding us, didn't you?"

"That's what my father always said."

"Look, Lévy paid me a fortune. They were all making up well-paid jobs for us in whatever businesses they ran, because they thought having the best players and winning trophies would be good for their companies. Those teams owned by Peugeot or Perrier, getting even richer off people like you, and me, telling everyone that we were ambassadors for them, because Lévy couldn't captain his country, could he? The Fédération were even worse – three weeks in South America just for travel expenses!"

"The honour wasn't enough?"

"I can't live on glory, can I?"

"If the money at Antibes was so bad, why did you leave Racing Club?"

"Someone lied about me to the police, saying I stole his business," said Villaplane, tears in his eyes. "I liked a drink and a night out, so everyone thought I must have, even though there was no proof. The police told me that if I paid them 400,000 francs and left Paris, they'd drop it. I asked Lévy if the club could pay but he said no, he'd heard too many stories about me. I had no choice: I gave them the money and went."

I took a deep breath. Villaplane glared at me.

"I don't have any money," I said, seeing the gun on his lap. "But if France win the war, then you're in big trouble." He shrugged. "Release me and I will speak in your favour."

"Promise?"

"I'm a Racing Club fan. Even though we lost, it was an honour to watch you in that cup final."

"I don't know how we didn't beat them," he said, finishing his cigar. "I can still see it – Cazal getting the better of me, then Friedmann breaking through…"

"It wasn't your fault. If everyone else had worked as hard as you then we'd have won."

"Perhaps," he said. "Cazal says I should have stayed at Sète, but those years in Colombes were the best of my career. Because of that, I will let you go."

We stood, and he shook my hand.

"When that game went to extra-time," I said, "You gave a speech. What did you say?"

"I just told everyone to keep going." He smiled at me, laughing at my disappointment. "What were you expecting?"

"Nothing," I said. We left the farmhouse via the back door. I saw the bodies of two peasants, shot and burned. Villaplane went through their pockets. He took some money, and a watch from one of their wrists. "Nice, isn't it? Do you want it?" I shook my head. "You sure? You could sell it." I stepped back. "I won't fire," he said. "Go!"

I walked away, and he returned to my comrades. "Shoot!" I heard, before eleven gunshots: none of them had 400,000 francs. I ran, wondering what became of the woman in the square.

★

I left for Paris that night, hitching lifts with sympathetic peasants who drove me as far as they could and then offered shelter. I arrived in August as the city celebrated its liberation, and joined the Forces of the Interior. Later that month, Villaplane was arrested. He had tried to hide at a farm, south of Paris, before escaping to Spain, but his gang was betrayed by a former member who exchanged his freedom for information on their whereabouts. Reprisals against collaborators were swift and brutal, but Villaplane and the heads of the *Carlingue* were not lynched. Instead, they were put on trial, beginning on 1 December.

It began with the formation of the gang. To establish themselves in Paris, the Nazis had linked up with black marketeers. Swiss national Max Stocklin, imprisoned as a German military informer, was released and got his contacts to free Henri Lafont, an illiterate whose criminal career began at 13, when his father died and his mother abandoned him. Lafont bought food, furniture, clothes, art and gold and sold them to the occupiers, opening bureaus for Jewish property and Norman livestock. He met bankers, lawyers and senior Nazis, some of whom felt the Reich's name was tarnished by association with such shabby crooks. So he infiltrated the Marseille Resistance, finding and torturing its Belgian leader, Lambrecht. This led to 600 arrests and Lafont getting license to tour Parisian prisons to recruit for his own operation.

Lafont's first choice was Pierre Bonny, a police officer who became famous in 1923, when Guillaume Seznec, head of a Morlaix sawmill, was convicted of killing business rival Pierre Quéméneur, condemned by a typewriter discovered in Bonny's investigation, which was apparently used to produce a false sales promise to lure Quéméneur into meeting Seznec. In 1934, Bonny helped to expose Alexandre Stavisky, who had sold 239 million francs' worth of false bonds from a pawn shop, buying off newspapers who tried to examine his affairs – this scandal caused far-Right riots that brought down the Republic's socialist government, and led to the conservative Doumergue becoming Prime Minister. Officially, Stavisky killed himself that January, but neither I nor anyone else had believed this, and it was rumoured that the police killed him due to his closeness to so many senior officials. The court didn't explore this further, though: it was more interested in Bonny's downfall in 1935, when he was charged with falsifying evidence in the Seznec case and jailed for three years – when he met Lafont.

Then, trembling, I realised: Bonny must have been part of the force that blackmailed Lafont's next recruit – Alexandre Villaplane. The court heard that Villaplane had no record of his parents other than that they were French, leaving the colony to move in with his uncles on the south coast aged 16. I thought back to that imperious first season at Racing Club as they discussed his football career, particularly its inglorious collapse at Antibes and his time in prison. After his release from prison in 1940, Lafont put him in charge of a bureau trading in gas, food and fine art, often procured from Jewish people. He specialised in smuggling gold and foreign currency, selling to and taking from anyone he could. In 1942, the Nazis recognised goods that he tried to sell to them, and he fled to Toulouse. After Cazal secured his return to Paris, the SS arrested him for stealing jewels. Lafont got him out: as the Nazis clamped down on the black market, he became Bonny's chauffeur and head of one of five BNA sections founded by Lafont, attaining the rank of *Untersturmführer*.

Villaplane stood. He looked far less comfortable than the other times I'd seen him in a suit, but as he took the dock, he steeled his shoulders, held out his chest and assumed that tone which I'd heard in that village square, and on that garage forecourt.

"I have been accused of betraying my nation," he said, putting his hand on his heart. "But anyone who likes football will know how much I love France, and how proud I was to captain my country – and it *was* my country. I got no education in Algeria, so I've always had to be a schemer, it's true. Especially in my career – was it fair that the best player in the land was not allowed to make a centime? Of course not! But as soon as it became legal to pay us, Lévy decided I was no longer of use to him, and I had to live on my wits. I made mistakes, I admit, but I was punished, and yet I knew that the Germans would want to kill me because of them – and that the only way to help my countrymen was to work with them."

His voice became louder, and I glanced around the court, trying to gauge who was convinced by his hand gestures, now wider and more frequent. "I stole from the Germans to give back to the French: for this I was even sent to the camp at Royallieu-Compiègne, with Resistance fighters and Jews. Would a committed Nazi be sent there, my friends? When I was released, I went to Périgueux. There, I would arrest members of the Resistance, telling my police chiefs not to shoot anyone until we'd found their weapons and we'd found out why family members had denounced each other, giving everyone else time to escape. Many came back to Périgueux to thank me, and by doing this, I saved more people than all of you in this court put together!"

He glanced at me, narrow-eyed, recognising me from Mussidan, and sat, to stunned silence. I tried not to return Villaplane's gaze even as it turned into a half-smile. A witness stood, describing the scene after Villaplane asked for money to save the villagers in the square. "Villaplane burst into the house of Geneviève Léonard, a 59-year-old mother of six accused of harbouring a Jew. His men ransacked it: He seized her hair, shouting "Where is your Jew?" She refused to answer, so he pushed her into the farm, hitting her with his rifle butt, and forced her to watch the BNA torturing two peasants. After being beaten and set on fire, they were shot. Alex laughed. Meanwhile, the BNA had located Antoine Bachmann, the Jew, and brought him over. Alex hit him and arrested him, ordering Léonard to give him 200,000 francs."

The bodies outside the farmhouse, I thought as I took the stand. "He stole from the peasants' corpses," I said. "He offered me money stolen from the pockets of the dead before I heard him give the order to shoot the maquisards at Mussidan, and although I was running away at the time, the bullets were fired so quickly that he must have pulled some of the triggers himself. I was spared as I support his old team, Racing Club. Because of that, I promised not to testify against him, but when I heard about Léonard, I knew I had to. As a boy, Alex was my hero, and I loved watching so much that I refused to believe those rumours about where he spent his money. But I should've done. He came to my father's garage and I got his autograph. It was the happiest day of my life. Then he talked my father into going into business with him, sold our property and kept the money. The police told me there was nothing they could do. So I wrote to Lévy, thinking that he might do something where nobody else would, and days later, Alex was sold to Antibes. I don't know if Alex knew M. Bonny back then, but I do know that just after Lafont got Alex out of prison, the police arrested my father and their gang killed him."

I looked back at Villaplane as I stood down: as he finally made the link between me and Lévy's decision to sell him, his shoulders dropped.

"Villaplane's psychology was different to the other members," said the prosecutor. "He himself admits that he is a schemer. I would say that he is a born conman, who seized the opportunity to get richer in a criminal society. Conmen have a sense that is indispensable to their trade – the sense for putting on a show. This is necessary for blinding their victims and getting them to give up what they want. He used it to commit the worst form of blackmail – the blackmailing of hope – throughout his life, exploiting the goodwill earned through his sporting brilliance, long after it allowed him to escape his difficult upbringing."

On the tenth day, the jurors spent 45 minutes deliberating. Judge Auguste Ledoux read the guilty verdict and sentenced Villaplane and eight of his eleven-man team to death for "intelligence with the enemy" – the twelfth, Edmond Delahaye, had died of acute diabetes in Fresnes prison the day before. Bonny burst into tears, weeping for his lost honour, as did Lafont and some of the others, for what their lives had been. As I looked at Villaplane, I remembered his despair when he realised that Racing Club were beaten in that cup final, fourteen years ago. He just stared, expressionless: he must have realised that there was nothing more to be gained from putting on a show, and perhaps, when the third goal went against us on that April afternoon at Colombes, he'd just been cursing the loss of Jean-Bernard Lévy's win bonus.

★

On 27 December 1944 at Fort de Montrouge, Alexandre Villaplane led out his squad for the last time, with Bonny and Lafont alongside him as if they were his half-back partners. Rather than a huge crowd at the national stadium, he lined up in front of the firing squad. Reading about it in the newspaper the next day, I could all but see Villaplane's eyes widen, almost certainly thinking of Montevideo as the order came to shoot.

WEEKEND IN BRIGHTON

1.

Patrick Berg – and today, as most days, he *was* Patrick, not Trish, he hardly ever got to be Trish, at least not outside his own head – walked down Buckingham Place towards the station. He stopped by the Belle Vue pub and stared across the hills, many terraced houses piled atop another. They'd started building a hotel, its white concrete a riposte to the glass of the new Jubilee Library. It had an LGBT section at least, even if it was no match for the University of Sussex's Queer Studies collection. Soon the view would be ruined.

The breeze hit his hairline, reminding him that it was starting to recede. *I should buy a wig,* he thought. *Maybe that shop in Hove will have something.* Then he thought about his overdraft, his student loan. Where would he find that fifty or sixty quid?

Not from work. He trudged across town towards his evening shift. He saw the *Argus* billboards at the station trying to be wacky. But cod-surrealist headlines like Mozart hip-hop makes grand master flash had felt less amusing ever since that moment two months ago when he had walked by and saw huge crowds, every train cancelled, the words Terrorists attack London offered by the local rag with uncharacteristic solemnity – a rare show of solidarity with the capital against which Brightonians often defined themselves.

He turned down Trafalgar Street. A portrait of John Peel had recently been painted on the side of the Albert, drawing attention away from the stencil of two policemen kissing just below, which he could never decide if he found charmingly romantic or tediously obvious. He looked wistfully at the second-hand bookshops, cafés and vintage clothes stores. He laughed at the young men in Trilby hats, and envied the women in polka-dot dresses, milling around the pubs in the mid-afternoon. He left the *Nathan Barley* types to their Shoreditch-on-sea and headed towards the office on Edward Street.

Patrick gazed at his office – the Wedding Cake, as it was known – all steel girders, blue tinted glass and forty-five-degree angles. *How could they waste such a dramatic building on something so bloody boring?* He swiped in, got the lift to the second floor, took his file from the shelf, found an empty desk, turned on the PC, and sat down.

PRESS CTRL + ALT + DELETE TO LOG IN

He unlocked the computer, saw the blue screen, got a coffee, came back and opened Outlook. **Inbox** (26). "Leaving drinks" from Rob in Accounts. "Just a reminder— King & Queen, 8pm." *No other plans,* thought Patrick. *Fuck it.* He typed, "I'll be there after I finish."

Now to waste five hours. He opened Internet Explorer and stared at the company homepage. *Probably best not to look for another job here, let alone dresses or shoes.* He clicked through his favourite haunts (*The Guardian*, B3ta, *Pitchfork*) and, finding nothing new, launched Excel. It had not become any more interesting since yesterday, but he had to at least look like he was working. He emailed the few other ex-student colleagues that he liked. He went to the canteen to buy snacks he didn't want. He went outside even though he didn't smoke. All the while he processed just enough new account forms to keep his line manager off his back for another evening.

It was getting dark as he left for the pub. *Oh God, Rob's into football,* he remembered as he fought through the guys in royal blue shirts. *And they're all looking at my hair.* He brushed it off his shoulder. He found his colleagues at a big table upstairs with pints of lager and salt and vinegar crisps, eyes on the match. There was little talk, mostly loud murmurs as the ball approached the goal. There was a discussion about Ray from Credit Control, who seemed to see David Brent from *The Office* as some sort of life coach. Lindsey was keen to reprise every detail of her daughter's recent wedding.

Patrick looked at his phone. *How long is it before it's socially acceptable to leave?* he wondered. He declined a drink and made an excuse.

"Already?" asked Rob, speaking to him for the only time that evening.

"Yeah... things to do tomorrow morning. Good luck in London."

He decided not to go home yet. He crossed back into Kemptown and drifted into the Queen's Arms, where he got a vodka and cranberry and sat in a corner. There were posters advertising drag queens but no entertainment tonight, and barely any clientele, just a couple of couples and a younger guy with bleached cropped hair who looked over and yelled, "Cheer up love, it might never happen!"

That sentence was always his cue to leave. He half-smiled, downed his drink and went outside. He wandered down towards Charles Street and R-Bar, the new joints by the seafront. A group of women in matching purple T-shirts were entering the latter. *Hen night on a Tuesday?* He turned back onto St. James's Street, where he tried the Bulldog. It was dark and even quieter than the last place, but he could tell that it was "butch" where the Queen's Arms had been "femme," as their names had suggested. The looks from the leather-clad skinheads were no more welcoming than the ones he'd got from the Chelsea fans in the King & Queen.

A flyer caught his eye. A man's face covered in red latex, black rubber circling the eye and mouth holes, in front of an attractive woman in a low-cut leather dress. *Divinity @ The Harlequin. Fetish lounge and dance club. Fetish or fantasy wear only.* Things ran through his mind, things he'd never told anyone about, or tried: serving a group of people at a party; being led on a chain, tied and gagged; having someone put him in the stocks and flog him...

Tickets were available from the sex shop near the station or Ashley's in Hove.

★

On Fridays, Patrick worked the early shift. He finished at 2pm and took the bus to New Church Road in Hove – the only journey he made in this town (it wasn't a 'city', no matter what the Council said) that was too far to walk.

The neurotically ordered grids of Hove, with their prosaic street names – First Avenue, Church Road – contrasted sharply with Brighton's higgledy-piggledy layout, an embodiment of the residents' snobbery: their insistence that they were from "Hove, actually," as that local in-joke had it. The small-c conservatism made it all the more surprising that Ashley's had opened here, but somehow it felt secluded near the end of the long boulevard, its signs and window display more discreet than the shops on St. James's Street, which targeted people with enough disposable income to clothe their dogs.

The door felt heavy. As he entered, he saw hangers of lingerie, red, black, white and soft pink, PVC nurses and maids' uniforms, a bin full of eyeliner and lipstick. At the counter there were books and magazines: *The Tranny Guide* and *Utterly Fabulous*, with impossibly beautiful people on their covers. A middle-aged man stood behind them, his clean-shaven face caked in foundation, brown eyes with a little mascara on the lashes.

"Can I help you?"

"Do you have any tickets for Divinity?"

"We've got a few." Patrick noticed that the assistant's hands were also shaved, with clear nail varnish. He moved his gaze to catch the assistant's eyes. They smiled at each other.

"How many did you want?"

"Just one."

"£15, please. What are you going to wear?"

"I don't know... I've got some heels, tights, a few dresses but I'm not sure they're right. I was thinking of buying a wig."

"We've got plenty of those."

Patrick saw stilettos, a room full of wigs on mannequin heads, some white boxes, open, with an array of false breasts, different sizes but all quite large, a few brown, mostly beige. He wondered if the silicone might feel nicer than cotton wool.

"What style were you after?"

"I don't know..."

"Hmm... I reckon light brown, not too long. Try these."

Patrick tried a brown wig in front of the mirror.

"I think the blonde highlights bring out your eyes."

"I love it," said Patrick.

"Now you'll need a dress." The assistant shot him a smile. "Are you a top or a bottom?"

"Huh?"

"Are you dominant, or submissive?"

Patrick said nothing.

"You look like a sub to me."

"How can you tell?"

"You're just a bit coquettish. Not rocket science, I know."

"But I don't want to tie myself to anything."

"No, but you want someone else to tie you to something."

They laughed awkwardly.

"Maybe just a little black dress, rather than a uniform," said the assistant, picking out a short cotton number with tassels on the arms and hemline. Patrick took off his shirt and trousers and tried it on over his bare chest and boxer shorts.

"Nice *legs*," said the assistant, gently rubbing his hand over Patrick's thighs as he pulled down the skirt.

"I'll take it," replied Patrick nervously. He quickly changed back into his work clothes.

"How long have you been here?" he asked as he handed over his debit card.

"Since 2001."

"Do you get much business?"

"We have a small core of loyal customers. I hope you'll become one."

"We'll see."

"Anyway, I'm Brian, or Bree," said the assistant. "And you?"

"Patrick. Uh, Trish."

"I'd have gone for Patricia. It's more ladylike." There was a pause. "Anyway, maybe I'll bump into you tomorrow night."

2.

Trish looked out at the collapsed remains of the West Pier, charred after two recent fires. Even though she knew that nobody could see through her window – at least not without a helicopter – she closed the blind. *Perhaps it would be fun to be more ladylike,* she thought as she went through the "female" side of her wardrobe. She went for the new dress with fishnet tights, a stuffed bra and her favourite knickers, black with an electric blue flower. No clip-on earrings, though: tonight, she hoped, there would be more enjoyable pains on offer. She put on pink lipstick and dark eye makeup, and then the wig.

She grinned as she moved the fringe into the right spot. She admired herself for a moment, repositioned her chest, pulled down the hemline of her dress. She threw her size 7½ black heels – with their narrow four-inch heels that she'd only walked in a couple of times, never successfully – into a charity shop handbag with her purse and keys, and put on flats. She dialled for a taxi, worrying about smudging her nails as she tapped out the number. She should have done them earlier.

She opened the front door and listened around the corridor. She was shaking slightly. Once she felt it was clear, she locked her flat and got the lift to the ground floor, keeping her head down to avoid conversation in case anyone else came in. Nobody did.

The driver stared, but, to her relief, didn't floor the accelerator.

"Where you going?"

"Providence Place. Just behind Woolworths on London Road."

Trish sat wordlessly as the driver took her along Western Road. She wondered how well she passed. Any conversation would betray her, she was sure. They turned left before they reached the crowds outside Churchill Square shopping centre, or the clubs and bars on West Street – "Fight Street," as her friends unaffectionately called it. They went down New England Road and into that shabby district around London Road, once the town's epicentre but now a run-down parade of second-hand shops and fast-food chains with the tired old Co-op Department Store at its ailing heart.

You never see this *on brochures or broadcasts about twenty-first-century Brighton.* They turned onto the dark, dank back street, and the driver pulled up outside the Harlequin. Trish changed into her heels and took a deep breath.

"Come on darling," said the doorman. "You'll catch a cold if you stand out here." She smiled at him and went in. She had been here a few times, but always in drab (as she called her male clothes) and usually on a weeknight, when she and her straight friends endured endless *Pussycat Dolls* or *Scissor Sisters* records in order to carry on drinking after the pubs closed. She had come only once on a Saturday night, to see a tired old drag queen belt out 'I Will Survive' before taking the piss out of the blouse she'd worn to an audience of about twenty.

Usually it was fairly quiet – another relic of a dying queer culture – but tonight the floor was packed with people in leather trousers, or PVC skirts and boots with tape over their nipples. The posters for the fifty-some-thing performers weren't visible as the house lights were down, although the disco lights around the bar broke the darkness for those wanting a drink. Tottering, struggling to make herself heard over the music – hard house, handbag, speedcore, she didn't know what – she tried to attract the attention of the guy behind the bar, who had piercings and a green Mohawk and was wearing a mesh T-shirt.

A woman next to her said hello. She had short, bleached hair and was dressed in red underwear with a collar and chain around her neck. An older man in leather was holding the end. Trish tried to look past her cleavage to the man's beard and half-naked torso, wondering what it might be like to spend the evening with them.

"Is this your first time?" the woman asked.

"Is it *that* obvious?" said Trish.

"Try to relax. Are you with anyone?"

"No."

"Oh, love. I'll buy you a drink. What'll you have?"

"Vodka and orange?"

The woman smiled at the barman, who served her next. The woman took her hand.

"Come upstairs with us," she said.

Trish followed the woman and her partner to the mezzanine floor. She gazed down over the banisters at the bar. A man in his underwear strapped to a St. Andrew's Cross was being gently flogged across his genitals. His eyes were shut, and he was yelping with each strike. Just below the empty dance floor, there were a few tables, each in a cubicle where little groups dressed in red or black hatched their plans. Next to them were the stocks, still unoccupied.

"Just going to get her warmed up," said the man to Trish, putting his partner's head and arms in place. He gently rolled up her skirt, put her underwear around her ankles and caressed her. *So much care and trust,* Trish thought as the man took a paddle and started spanking the woman. She recalled some of her adolescent fantasies. *The little pats between the strikes must be the most exciting bit.*

Someone tapped her shoulder. "You like that?" It was a woman in a red latex dress with matching gloves and boots, brown wavy hair, hazel-coloured eyes and deep red lips, holding a whip.

"Wanna go next?"

Fuck. Trish looked down at her dress. *She'll know that you like her...* She held her bag in front of her waist coyly, and took another breath. "Go on, then. If I *must*."

"I'm Candy."

Candy handed the whip to Trish. She gave it straight back. Candy raised her eyebrows; Trish grinned, trying not to blush, as the man let his partner out of the stocks and took her downstairs.

Trish let Candy take her hand and put it through one of the holes. She gave Candy her other arm, and then bowed her head so that Candy could fix it in place. Candy bolted down the top, rolled up Trish's skirt, pulled down her underwear and spread her legs further apart.

Trish closed her eyes and listened to Candy step back. She clenched her teeth until the whip cracked across her buttocks. *Yeow!* More strikes, each more painful and pleasurable than the last. Candy leant into her, driving her nails and elbows into her back, kicking her thighs and laughing as she lost her footing. Just as Trish began to wish she would stop, Candy stroked her behind and then walked around the stocks to face her.

"Are you okay, darling?"

Trish nodded.

"Shall I carry on?"

"Yes, please."

Candy kissed her on the cheek and then struck her hard with the whip. Six more lashes were enough: Trish stamped her foot to get Candy's attention, and then asked her to stop. Candy pulled up Trish's underwear, put her skirt down and released her, giving her a hug.

Someone was coming towards her: middle-aged, with brown eyes, wearing a crushed velvet dress and a black wig, cut into a bob.

"It's Bree – we met at Ashley's. I *knew* you'd make a gorgeous girl!"

Trish smiled, doing a half-ironic curtsy.

"How are you?"

"Sore!"

Bree laughed.

"It's nice, isn't it?" Trish smiled again and nodded.

"Wanna swap?" Bree said.

"You want me to spank you?"

"Why not? You might enjoy it."

Will I? wondered Trish. *I've always been sub...*

"Come on, use this." Candy interrupted and slapped a paddle into Trish's hand. "I'll tell you what to do."

"Come on then." Trish tried awkwardly to return Bree's beaming grin. *If it makes her happy.* She took Bree's hand and led her to the stocks, copying what Candy had done to her. She gently patted Bree's backside and then smacked it hard.

"Move up and down," said Candy, "and aim for the top of her leg." Trish kept going. "Check that she's okay, and show her some tenderness, too."

Trish asked Bree if she was all right. Bree nodded, and Trish went back to hitting her, a little more enthusiastically each time.

"Mistress! Mistress!" she heard over the music.

Mistress! How exciting!

"I'd like to stop now."

"Okay, hon," said Trish. "Let me buy you a drink."

Trish handed the paddle back to Candy, let Bree out, gave her a hug, kissed her on the cheek and took her downstairs.

The crowd around the bar had thinned out as the dance floor had filled. They took the only empty seats, in the corner, by the jukebox. Trish half-smiled at Bree, struggling to work out what to say.

"How long have you worked at Ashley's?"

"Sorry?"

Trish leaned over, raising her voice.

"How long have you worked at Ashley's?"

"Oh – just over a year. Part-time."

"What else do you do?"

"What?"

"I said, what else do you do?"

"Sorry love, I can't hear you," said Bree, pointing at the speaker above them. "I'm a decorator. Why don't we go back to my hotel? We can chat there."

"Okay, sure."

Bree called a taxi. They finished their drinks and went out to the car.

"St. George's Terrace, please."

The driver nodded.

"Hope you're not too sore," said Bree.

Trish half-smiled.

"Where do you live?"

"Embassy Court," she replied.

"That manky old tower on the seafront?"

"They're doing it up," said Trish. "Fixing the broken windows and cleaning the grime off the front. I'll probably have to move out once they're done, though."

Silence.

"How come you're at a hotel?"

"I live in Crawley," said Bree. "Moved into a one-bed place after I broke up with my wife. The kids are with her in Three Bridges."

"Was that because…"

Bree nodded.

"Oh sweetheart, I'm sorry," said Trish, taking Bree's hand.

"It's all right," Bree replied, betraying the opposite with her eyes.

"Do you want to go all the way?"

"I'm too old now, and the boys have been through enough," said Bree. "What about you?"

"I don't know. I probably would, if it wasn't so much effort."

Bree laughed.

"Are you with anyone?"

"No, I'm single," replied Trish. "I'm always single."

"Well, then, at least you don't have that to worry about."

"Yes, I suppose."

They reached the hotel. Bree led Trish through the empty reception and up the stairs.

The wallpaper in the room was that orangey-brown shade with hexagonal patterns that she had last seen in pubs on soap operas in the early 1990s. It absorbed the light from the flickering bulb after Bree turned on the bedside lamp, and somehow made the room feel even darker, and just a little sadder. Bree drew the blinds, stained and beige. Trish sat in the chair by the desk, looking at her hands.

Bree picked up her jeans, removed the belt and gave it to Trish. She put her hands on the bed and leant over.

"Oh," said Trish. "I thought you just wanted to chat."

"We'll have plenty of time for that," replied Bree. "Go on."

Trish hesitated, and then moved behind Bree, and cracked the belt with a loud whoosh.

"Won't people hear us?" she whispered.

"It'll be all right. I'm only here until tomorrow morning," replied Bree.

"What if they knock?"

"It'll be *fine*. It's still quite early, anyway."

Trish swung the belt again. There wasn't enough space: it kept striking the wardrobe, the wall or the bedpost, draining its force well before it got to Bree.

"Use your hand, I'll lie across your lap." Trish sat on the bed, and Bree laid across her. "Roll up my skirt."

Trish suppressed a sigh, and sensed Bree becoming impatient, wriggling a little across her lap. She followed Bree's request and spanked her a few times.

"Harder."

She hit Bree with more force and then looked at the door. "I thought I heard someone."

"If you're really not comfortable, we can stop," said Bree.

"It's just... you're too *nice*. I feel bad about hurting you."

"You managed it earlier."

"It's different in a club." Trish suppressed a tear. "You seem really sweet, but ..."

Bree sat up and put her hand on Trish's knee. They both left it there for a moment. Bree moved to kiss her. Trish backed away slightly, shifted her head and put her arms around Bree.

"I'm sorry, darling." She held Bree tighter. "I'm sorry."

She let go. "It's late. I should leave."

"You won't walk along the seafront, will you?"

"No, I'll get too much shit off people. There's a taxi rank up the road."

"Here," said Bree, tearing a page from a notebook and picking up a pen. "There's a website called TV-TS World. My username is Breanna. Find me on there if you ever want to chat."

"I will."

Trish took the note, put it in her bag, hugged Bree and left. *Why am I so disappointed? I've finally met someone like me, tried something I've always wanted to try...* Whatever lay beneath it would have to wait. She was too tired to think about it now. She got out her Discman, put in the earphones and started *Chicks on Speed*'s 'Glamour Girl' as she went through reception. Even though it felt laughably inappropriate, she kept the music on. It would drown out any heckles as she walked home. She didn't want to shell out on another taxi. She kept her head down along the promenade, feeling – correctly – that the dark would protect her, and that none of the people coming out of the clubs would scrutinize her too closely.

At home she turned on her laptop, looked at the topics on the forum that Bree recommended – mainly about where to buy makeup or clothes, but there were also bitter arguments about newspaper articles, TV sketch show *Little Britain* and a new film called *Transamerica* – and decided not to register.

Soon after, the Harlequin closed, Divinity seemed to disappear, and she got a letter telling her that her rent would increase. When she decided to try her luck in London, she momentarily wondered what became of Rob in Accounts. She never saw Bree again.

THE ART OF CONTROL

Tamara O'Hara woke at noon to see an envelope lodged in her letterbox, overshadowing the boots, corsets, whips and chains piled by the door to her studio flat after a video shoot.

16 April 2015

Dear sir/madam,

Re: www.tamara-tv-takeover.co.uk ("the Service")
As you may be aware, following amendments to the Communications Act 2003, UK providers of video on demand services operating on or after 1 December 2014 have been obliged to notify these services to us, The Authority for Television and Video On Demand Ltd ("ATVOD").

ATVOD has received a complaint regarding the Service identified above, and we are writing to you as you appear to be the provider. This letter is to inform you that we are investigating the Service for potential breaches of ATVOD's rules 1, 4 and 11, corresponding to the requirements of the Communications Act 2003 ("the Act") as below:

Rule 1: Requirement to notify an on-demand programme service (section 368BA of "the Act")
Rule 4: Requirement to pay a fee (Section 368(E)(3) (ZA) of the Act)
Rule 11: Requirement to ensure that children will not normally see or hear material which might seriously impair their development (Section 368(E) (2) of the Act)

ATVOD has been designated by Ofcom [*the Office of Communications*] **as the co-regulator for on demand programme services under the Communications Act 2003, as amended by the Audiovisual Media Services Regulation 2009 and the Audiovisual Media Regulations 2010.**

She had been expecting *something* like this since the law changed, and she'd read about what could no longer be shown in online pornography: peeing and *female* ejaculation (if performed onto another person and/or consumed); fisting; full bondage with a gag; 'age play'; sex at gunpoint (if 'believable'); anything liable to cause more than 'transient and trifling' pain, e.g. spanking, caning or whipping; face-sitting (if performed by a woman on a man); trampling; verbal abuse; numerous other acts, some that she'd never tried ('Power Tools' sounded best left to the professionals), some that she and her queer friends enjoyed, all banned on the basis that they could harm viewers who copied them, or children who saw them.

She scanned the letter, wondering if her site fitted their definition of a UK-based On Demand Programming Service, or if she had 'editorial responsibility'. She checked her phone: they had emailed a copy, so she forwarded it to a client who worked as a lawyer.

'Rob – just got this from ATVOD. Do they expect normal people to be able to understand it??'

The reply came within five minutes.

'They think you're a TV on demand site providing things they want to ban. They're asking you to prove you're not – if you can't then you'll have to register – pay an annual fee for them to censor you. Good news though – they offer 'concessionary rates for non-commercial and small-scale providers' below their usual flat fee. Nice of them, isn't it? Call if you want to chat x'

Tamara phoned Rob.

"How are we going to fight these fuckers, then?"

"You need to respond now. You're supposed to get nine days before you lose the right to reply, but this has turned up three days before the deadline. The best thing to do first is to tell them that you're not a TV on demand service, but it's hard to argue that you're not competing with BBC iPlayer or Channel 4 on Demand when your site is called *Tamara's TV Takeover*."

"They're not competing with *me*," shouted Tamara. "I give my customers something they've not had since Channel 4 stopped the Red Triangle! Tell Mary Whitehouse or whoever sent this that I make *art*, not porn."

"We could give it a shot. I'm happy to draft a letter saying as much. I can quote that transgender fisting scene in *Ulysses* as a work of literary merit, although it's pretty tame compared to some of your stuff."

"Of course it is, it's a hundred years old. Mention all the queer filmmakers – Warhol and that. Tell them about the police shutting down *Flaming Creatures* by Jack Smith but Susan Sontag saying it was beautiful, and ask why it's alright to show *Blow Job* in a cinema but not for me to put *Perv Your Enthusiasm* on my tiny little website."

"I can tell you why," said Rob. "It's because cinemas

make sure children don't see it. Their concern is about payment – you take money from debit cards, which under-18s can use."

Tamara's eyes widened.

"Christ, am I going to have to take everything down?"

"It might be worth restricting your Members' Area until this is sorted."

"But this could take months! How am I going to make the rent?"

"Do more sessions with clients?"

"I want to make films – not just do whatever some City cunt asks for, even if I tell myself I'm making the bankers pay for the crisis every time I whip them. And I can't even do that when they're wanking behind a webcam." Rob laughed. "I've got an idea. Send me the letter when it's done – they probably won't accept it, but it'll stall them while I get my shit together."

Tamara text messaged three people: Maria, another dominatrix who often featured in the videos she put on her site, and on a download service called Films4You; Chris, who she called "my favourite sub"; and Harmony, who provided and operated a digital camera.

'Are you around over the next few weeks? May have a project for you xxx'

They replied quickly: they were around, and intrigued. 'Cool,' wrote Tamara. 'I'll be in touch.'

★

A few weeks later, Rob sent an email to Tamara, simply headed 'Bad news.' Attached was a scan of a letter from ATVOD:

The Service is in ATVOD's view an On Demand Programme Service ("ODPS") which offers strong fetish adult material …

'Don't bother reading all of it,' wrote Rob. 'Gist of it is that they *do* think you're a TV on demand service. We'll have to take this up a level – appeal to OFCOM.'

'Okay,' replied Tamara. 'We're going to send them a film.'

That Saturday morning, Tamara put some plants and posters around the flat, trying to make it look like a set for a television programme. Maria, Chris, and Harmony arrived just after noon, and Tamara explained the premise.

"Harmony, I want you to film. Everyone has approved my scenario – from there we're going to improvise, like an Andy Warhol movie. Maria – you and I start as TV presenters on the sofa, in our power suits, me in red, you in blue. We're doing a show called *Live in Your Living Room* – a bit like *EuroTrash,* but more hardcore."

"Which channel?" laughed Maria.

"It doesn't matter," replied Tamara. "Something on Sky, late at night. Anyway – we're talking about how we're being shut down. Then Chris comes in. He's one of the regulators, here to explain the new rules."

Maria and Tamara put their hands on their hips, smiling at Chris. He laughed nervously, putting on the suit that Tamara had told him to wear.

"What'll we do with him?" asked Maria, licking her lips.

"We let him explain," said Tamara. "Then we kidnap him. Here's a gun." She handed a replica weapon to Maria. "We take him to a secret location and tell him that either he gets the ATVOD laws revoked, or he becomes our slave." She looked at Chris. "Which will it be?"

"We'll see," he replied, laughing.

"So, we're starting and we don't know how it's going to end," said Tamara. "It's like *Casablanca,* isn't it? Maria – you sit on the sofa, next to me. Do your make-up while Harmony sets up the camera, and then we'll start chatting."

"We're rolling," whispered Harmony.

Tamara: Hello, and welcome to *Live in Your Living Room*, with me, Tamara O'Hara, and my co-host and lover Maria Marx. I'm afraid this might be our last show – the government are trying to ban anything that shows women in control.

Maria: *[Tugs on her blue jacket]* And to think I modelled myself on Maggie.

Tamara: Let's be clear on the new legislation. It targets acts popular within the queer and S&M communities and tries to undermine the very basis of female pleasure, let alone domination. You're not allowed to show a woman "blocking the airways" of a man, with a strap-on or something, but showing a man doing that to a woman with his penis is fine. You're allowed to show a man coming, but not a woman.

Maria: So it's an act of state censorship?

Tamara: It looks like it. And you might think that if the Conservatives want to make British politics more like America's, where the religious right have more influence, then banning depictions of the most radical sex acts might be where they'd start.

Maria: Do they make any allowances for the fact that spanking, caning and humiliation might be consensual, or not?

Tamara: Absolutely none. There was no consultation with any producers, and the organisation responsible has been totally unaccountable. Until tonight, as we have a special guest – Gideon McGill, Chief Executive of the Authority for Television and Video On Demand services. He's going to tell us exactly what this means for our show, and our friends in the fem-dom industry. *[To audience]* Don't boo, it'll only make them angrier!

Gideon sits on the armchair, next to the sofa.

Tamara: Gideon, can you explain why these rules have been introduced?

Gideon: It's not a conspiracy to outlaw female pleasure, or power. We simply want to stop children being able to access material that may harm them.

Tamara and Maria stand and pull their guns on him.

Tamara: It's always about the fucking *children*, isn't it?

Tamara addresses the camera, holding her gun across her chest.

Tamara: We are taking him hostage – Gideon will be our gimp until the laws are abolished. ATVOD: you know where you can contact us.

Tamara put down her arm and laughed.

"Okay, that's scene one. I'll add some crowd noises and a title card saying we've taken him to our dungeon. Let's set up for the next one. Harmony – put some light in the corner where the chair is. And you," she said, handing Chris a latex suit and face mask with spiked collar, "put this on. We'll open with us tying you up."

Chris changed into his costume and sat. Tamara and Maria got into leather boots with 5" heels, fishnet stockings, leather miniskirts, black crop tops and balaclavas, before Tamara gave Harmony the signal to shoot.

Tamara: Here's some regulation that you *won't* like.

Tamara straps Gideon's ankles to the chair and cuffs his hands behind his back.

Gideon: We will *not* give in to terrorism! The government will-

Maria: Oh, shut up.

Maria fastens a ball gag over Gideon's mouth. She draws her gun and stands next to the chair, before the camera. Tamara reads from a sheet of paper.

Tamara: Here are our demands. First: the abolition of the new legislation and dissolution of ATVOD. We will continue to disobey until the law is revoked – full bondage and a gag for our captive will just be the start. Next: regulation of sexual material to be conducted by those who understand and respect the female orgasm. Finally, the revolution – as prophesised by Shulamith Firestone and Valerie Solanas.

"Okay, well done," said Tamara to Chris, untying him. "Next, it's the fun bit. You worshipping us. Strip naked, get down, then put your arms around my bum and your face up against my pussy." Chris obeyed, and Tamara winked at Harmony.

Tamara: On your knees, slave.

Maria pushes into the shot and strokes her strap-on against

Gideon's mouth.

Maria: Let's make him gag.

Tamara: No — let's make him *read*. He might learn something.

Tamara puts a book in Gideon's hands and holds a gun to him.

Tamara: This is *Public Sex: The Culture of Radical Sex* by Pat Califia. Read the passage I've highlighted. For every mistake, every hesitation, I will punish you. Actually, I might just punish you anyway.

Gideon starts reading.

Gideon: Three years ago, I decided to stop ignoring my sexual fantasies.

Tamara: *[Grabs Gideon's hair]* To the *camera,* you idiot!

Gideon: Since the age of two, I had been constructing a private world of dominance, submission, punishment and pain. Abstinence, consciousness-raising, and therapy have not blighted the charm of these fearful revelries. I could not tolerate any more guilt, anxiety, or frustration, so I cautiously began to experiment with real sadomasochism. I did not lose my soul in the process. But in those three years, I lost a lover, several friends, a publisher, my apartment and my good name because of the hostility and fear evoked by openness about my true sexuality.

Tamara slaps Gideon, making him drop the book. She slaps him again as he tries to pick it up. Then she grabs him by the hair, pulls him over to the chair, bends him over and spanks him with a paddle. After ten strikes, she stops.

Tamara: That's enough for now. You know your options. Abolition of the ATVOD laws, or life as our slave. Which is it to be?

Gideon: I can't put my life above the well-being of our children. If I have to sacrifice myself – so be it!

Maria: I think he *wants* to be our prisoner.

Tamara: We'll soon find out.

Tamara puts on a strap-on near Gideon's mouth. He shakes his head. Tamara holds the gun to his face and he relents. Maria walks around and puts her strap-on into his behind.

Gideon: *[Removing Tamara's strap-on, after two minutes]* Alright, I'll get the law scrapped!

Tamara and Maria high-five each other across his body.

Maria: Promise?

Gideon: Promise!

Tamara puts her strap-on back into his mouth and then carries on for another two minutes. Then she walks over to the camera.

Tamara: You heard us – the law is to be abolished. We shall release the hostage when we get written confirmation from ATVOD. It is in his interest for you to announce the dissolution of your organisation. We shall continue to punish our slave for crimes against people engaged in consensual sexual practices until we receive this announcement.

Tamara and Maria tie Gideon to the chair and gag him.

"Okay, that's a wrap," said Tamara, taking the gag out of Chris's mouth.

"Leave it in for a while," he replied, laughing.

"I think you've had enough for now. Anyway, I need to start editing. Well done guys, and thanks. It'll be online soon, I'll send the link to you. And our friends at ATVOD, of course."

★

Tamara finished editing. She disabled all the links on her site – About, Videos, Photos, Sessions, and Contact Me – and created a new home page.

Tamara's TV Takeover
Do Not Adjust Your Set
The Authority for TV and Video On Demand
services is trying to shut us down – or at least stop us
having any fun. This film is our communication to them.
Due to explicit sexual content,
it should not be viewed by under-18s.

She went on Twitter.

Tamara TV @tamara_takeover · 29 April
Our film in response to #ATVOD and #OFCOM is up!
We have sent it to them – watch it here: tamara-tv-
takeover.co.uk/home #DoNotAdjustYourSet

She emailed the link to Rob.

'Here's the film. I've scanned a ransom note made from cut up newspapers, too, telling them to meet our demands. Send it all to OFCOM, asking them to review the material when they make their judgement. Tell them it's fucking *art*, not just TV – let alone porn. If they want a fight, I'm up for it.'

'Will do x' replied Rob, and she waited for the adjudication.

★

A month later, Rob wrote back to Tamara.

SUBJECT: Appeal to OFCOM
'Great news – you can keep going! But you might not like their logic... x'

She opened the attached letter and read past the verdict to their reasoning.

'It is the opinion of OFCOM that Tamara's TV Takeover does not constitute a TV On Demand service, as the material is not of sufficient quality, technically or aesthetically. The production is crude and amateurish, poorly lit and badly shot; the plotline is minimal and not believable, whilst the dialogue is stilted and the acting under-rehearsed. OFCOM feel that this content is of no artistic merit, and so should be exempted from ATVOD regulation.'

Furious, Tamara threw the letter to the floor. *They said the same about Jack Smith,* she thought, *and James Joyce.* She picked it up, put it in a drawer and started planning her next film – one that would explore her feelings about securing freedom of speech, but only for herself.

CORRIDORS OF POWER

At the peak of the band's fame in 1985, Trevor Horn and Paul Morley of ZTT Records licensed a video game based on *Frankie Goes to Hollywood*. Several 8-bit renditions of their hits served as soundtracks for an oblique adventure, where you had to help 'Frankie' escape Mundanesville (a network of suburban houses) and enter the 'Pleasuredome'.

Whatever the Pleasuredome was, it could only be accessed once you had a personality score of 99%, completing challenges that raised your standing in Sex, War, Love and Religion. In one house in Mundanesville, you would find a dead body. Clues would appear, such as 'The killer is a socialist' and 'Joe Public has always voted Tory': eventually you could identify the culprit, providing some of the 87,000 Personality Points needed to complete the game.

You could play videos on the televisions, and sub–games would pop up. In one, you could be either Reagan or Gorbachev, and you had to win a spitting battle. (I always picked Gorbachev.) In another, you had to shoot celebrities – Reagan, Thatcher and others I didn't recognise. Elsewhere, you had to stop Merseyside being bombed, or collect flowers, with several vignettes accessible from the Terminal Room.

I loved the hermetic feel of playing games into the night, sealed from the prying eyes of small-minded suburbia. 'Frankie' was my favourite, and the Terminal Room felt like its heart, insulated from the rest of its world, just the bleeps and dials of the mainframe and four smaller computers for company. Only one door in Mundanesville was locked: behind it were the Corridors of Power, a maze-like network with exits to every game. Once you found the key, you could navigate them: this was the game's *centre,* leading ultimately to the Pleasuredome.

★

Manja and I left Cinema 1 at the Institute of Contemporary Arts, not staying to applaud.

"That wasn't much, was it?" I said.

"He doesn't like the internet," replied Manja, "I *get* it."

"The best advice I ever got was 'Beware the long synopsis.' It says: 'Witty and insightful films about how technology has warped our communications, old media melting into new ones in unpredictable, unprecedented ways.'We get fifteen minutes of a bloke checking Facebook."

"Drink?"

The artist, known only as Stevo, stood by the bar, lapping up the congratulations. Those too drunk or too normcore for his inner circle settled for talking to us. The usual questions:

Where are you from?

"Flitwick," I said. "Bedfordshire."

"Ljubljana," replied Manja. "Slovenia."

Are you artists?

"I work in digital video," Manja replied. "Frankie is an arts journalist."

"And a courier," I said.

Oh, that must be interesting.

"I go to all sorts of places. But I only see the façades."

Where do you live, and how do you get by in London?

"We're in a warehouse in Seven Sisters," said Manja, "with five other people. It's not great, but we manage."

Finally, inevitably: *Are you a couple?*

I gave Manja a beat, and then: "No, we're just house-mates. We lived together at Central St. Martin's and now we're in the same place again."

I saw a familiar face walk towards the bar. That face broke into a huge grin, and then its owner starting wagging both of her index fingers at us in happy recognition.

"Oh God, it's Claude."

"Yes," said Manja. "And she's wasted."

"Do you know those guys she's with?"

"Do I ever?"

"Did *you* invite her?" I whispered.

Manja shook her head, scowling.

"Hey guys, how are *youuuuuuu?*" Without waiting for our reply, she introduced us to Adam and Andrew. "They're *art dealers,*" she declared, not looking at the middle-aged men in suits alongside her. Then she turned, telling them to "meet Frankie and Manja, from my degree."

"Oh, hi," said Manja. "Sorry, but we were just thinking of going."

"Oh, come on!" begged Claude.

"I've got to get up early tomorrow..." I said.

"They promised to buy us drinks," replied Claude, as Andrew and Adam looked at each other.

"Alright," I said. "If you insist."

"Don't sound too enthusiastic."

"I didn't."

"What are you having?"

"White wine."

"Get a bottle, yeah?" said Claude, waving her hand.

We sat down. Claude poured her glass first, more generous than ours. I looked at Manja but we knew this wasn't worth contesting; we exchanged several more glances as Claude talked loudly about selling two of her 'Intimate Self-Portraits', spending the money on champagne and taxis to parties, telling us which of the 1990s artists who Manja and I hated had given her which drugs, and when.

Claude went to the toilet.

I whispered to Manja: "What should we do?"

"Get the bus."

I nodded. Adam and Andrew asked us about where we were from, if we were artists, where we lived in London and how we got by, before Claude returned with another bottle.

"Claude, *no!*" said Manja.

"Oh, you're so uptight… you Slovakians."

"Slovenians."

"I know, you keep telling me," Claude replied, filling our glasses. Manja glared at her. "If you *really* don't want it, I'll have it."

Claude drank from Manja's glass. Manja took Claude's.

"Hey, that's mine!" said Claude.

"And that's *mine.*"

They stopped, laughed, clinked the glasses and carried on drinking.

"Where are you going next?" said Claude.

"*Home,*" I replied.

"I was asking *them,*" Claude informed me, turning to Andrew and Adam.

"We're meeting our friends at a club."

"Come on," said Manja. "We're leaving."

"We should go too," replied Andrew, getting up.

We went outside. Manja and I walked up The Mall towards Trafalgar Square, before turning to see Claude going in the other direction with the two men.

"Oh, for *fuck's sake…*"

"We can't leave her," said Manja, walking quickly after them.

"Where are we going?" asked Claude.

"Annabel's," replied Adam.

"What's that?" said Claude.

"It's a private members' club," Andrew told us, "named after Annabel Goldsmith. Been there for fifty years – everyone who's anyone is a member."

"We're not," Manja said.

"Don't worry, we'll get you in. Your friend might need to smarten up, though."

"Is it far?"

"Ten minutes' walk."

"We're *leaving*," said Manja.

"Give it a chance," implored Claude.

"Let's give it half an hour," I suggested, curious to see inside such a famous club.

"*What?*" Manja replied.

"It'll be an experience."

"Being surrounded by poshos?"

"You were happy to dress up for those art twats," said Claude. "Mr Curator, notice *me!*"

We reached Berkeley Square in silence. The first thing we noticed was how tall the trees were, their summer greens irresistibly beautiful. We walked past the railings around the park, locked at night, and stared up at the penthouses above the five or six-storey blocks of flats.

"If I was Damien Hirst, I'd buy one of these," I told Manja, laughing.

"Have you ever delivered here?"

"I can't remember. These places all look the same."

Adam and Andrew went down some steps, towards a

basement. Claude grabbed my hand and dragged me after them. I raised my eyebrows at Manja, who grudgingly followed.

The doorman, dressed in a discreet black suit, sized us up.

"These your guests?" Adam and Andrew nodded. "Your friend really should wear a jacket," he told them, looking at me.

"What if I tuck in my shirt and do up my top button?" I replied.

"You still need a jacket, sir."

As Adam and Andrew entered, Claude touched the doorman's arm.

"Come on," she said. "We've come all the way from Croydon for this."

"We walked ten–"

Claude shot Manja her *shut up* look that we both knew so well.

"Croydon?" said the doorman. "I *say*, we *can't* let the riff-raff in."

"It's alright, we're Londoners," replied Claude, using a tone that left me unsure if she was playing along with his joke, or genuinely offended.

"Londoners or not, he still needs a jacket," said the doorman. "Ask at the cloakroom if they've got a spare. If anyone asks you about it, you'll have to leave."

He waved us through. The cloakroom attendant greeted us with a smile.

"The doorman told me to borrow a jacket," I said. "Do you have any lying around?"

"Just this," the attendant replied, handing me a black one, I presumed from lost property. "It's a medium. Leave your bags, coats, phones and cameras here, please."

I thanked the attendant and put on the jacket, finding

it a little tight. Claude threw her bags at us to check in and did her make-up in the huge mirror, opposite the toilets. We followed her past the bar to the lounge, where an elderly couple were drinking.

"They're staring at us," said Manja.

"Then ignore them and get pissed, I'm paying."

"You sure?" laughed Manja, but Claude had already gone.

I slumped into one of the red velvet chairs, by the fireplace, noticing how the dim lighting bounced off the mustard-yellow walls.

"Are you okay?"

"I think I have Stendhal syndrome."

"He got that from looking at masterpieces in Florence," Manja told me. "Not from a few tacky paintings of dogs."

Before I could answer, we heard a voice from the bar: *"How much?"*

"Our whites start at £25," said the barman, "with the Garnacha Blanco."

"Fine, whatever," Claude replied.

Before we could stop Claude, she had a bottle and three glasses. *Your money,* I thought as she handed over her debit card.

"It's dead down here," she shouted. She marched towards the stairs, so we followed. On our left was a white door. Claude tried to enter, but it was locked. She knocked. No response.

"Leave it," said Manja.

Claude knocked again, and then tried to pull the door open. The barman looked up at us.

"Excuse me, madam – that room is private."

"Didn't want to go in there anyway," replied Claude, before stumbling upstairs.

At the top of the stairs, Manja and I gasped as we saw

the indoor garden. The domed ceiling was decorated with fairy lights, a cheap imitation of the night sky; a few bulbs flickered and failed. I could hear water flowing but I couldn't tell where it was. The walls were covered in decking and green vines, with pot plants around the edges, all immaculately groomed, with patrons sat on purple and pink chairs around little tables with candles. By the bar, a group of men in brown or black dinner jackets stood smoking cigars.

"I feel like I'm in a bad Fellini film," I said to Manja.

"Why do they all stand like that?" she asked, noting that they had their legs slightly apart.

"Assertiveness training, probably," I replied.

One took a long draw and blew out the smoke, with a contemptuous nod towards us. I glanced over at Claude, who had introduced herself to two men, tilting her head with laughter.

"Are you alright?" asked Manja.

"Yeah," I replied. "I just hate rich people."

"What do you think these guys do for a living?"

"Estate agents, solicitors, bankers," I replied.

"Arms dealers, maybe," said Manja, half-laughing.

"I met someone recently who specialised in Asset of Community Value cases," I said. "She was one of the highest-paid lawyers in Britain, or so she kept saying. Anyway, landlords and property developers would hire her to challenge anyone who claimed that they were good for local people, to make it easier to kick them out. Honestly, how would you sleep at night?"

"You'd climb into bed, and when your husband asks, 'What did you do today?' you'd say, 'I closed down three arts organisations, two pubs and a children's playground.' Then you'd be out like a light."

As we started laughing, Claude came over.

"Not talking to anyone, then?"

"No, we're alright," I said.

"You two are so closed-minded!"

"These people run *everything,*" replied Manja. "What could we possibly learn from them?"

"Nothing, with *that* attitude," Claude insisted. "Come and meet Martin, you'll like him."

Claude grabbed my hand and yanked me across the room.

"What do you do?" I asked, to break the silence.

"I make programmes for assurance firms so they can check that people are paying the right tax," declared Martin.

"They should check everyone here first," I said to Manja, before Claude kicked me in the shin. Too late, as Martin had heard. He shook his head, picked up his bag and left.

"Proud of yourself, Frankie?" asked Claude. "Coming into their club and bullying them?"

"*Bullying* them?" I replied. "These bastards take over our galleries, turn our studios into luxury flats, wipe out all the jobs that we might take to sustain ourselves and charge us hundreds a month for a fucking shoebox in fucking Ilford, but joking about their taxes is bullying?"

Then I realised that everyone was staring at us.

"We'd better go," whispered Manja.

I headed out, quietly. Claude pushed ahead of us, back down the stairs. She took a key from her purse, holding it up with a grin – I guessed that she'd swiped it from Martin's table – and opened the white door.

"Haha, nice one!" I said. Manja raised her eyebrows, impressed. And then we saw a large room, with twelve people sat around a long table. On the walls were several oil paintings, all dead white men, probably from the 19th century. The table was laid out for dinner, the finest china, but there was no food. At the far end was a computer screen, covering the entire wall. On it were some graphs, dropping across the X axis, below the heading Profit Margins 14-15.

As Claude pulled out a chair from under the table, I noticed that again, everyone was glaring at us – the men were in black tie, the women in ball gowns. As Manja whispered, "This is it?" the man by the screen said: "Excuse me – who invited you here?"

"Adam and Andrew," replied Claude, smiling at them.

"Did you?" asked the chair.

"No," they answered in unison.

"We met you at the ICA," said Claude. "You promised you'd get us in."

"Into the *club*," stammered Andrew. "Not in here…"

Claude winked at me.

"What are you lot doing, anyway?" I asked. "I thought you'd be having one of those parties where the Prime Minister has sex with a pig. Instead it's just spreadsheets."

"Initiations do not happen here," said an elderly man, before his companion elbowed him.

"We try not to combine business and pleasure in the dining room, but they're so hard to separate nowadays," one of the few women told us.

"What's wrong with enjoying our work?" asked the chair. "Now, please explain who you are."

"We're artists," said Manja.

The room went quiet. The diners looked at each other, nervously. Someone coughed. The chair of the meeting banged the table.

"Next on the agenda is the Arts Council, and how to abolish it," he said, grinning at us.

"I wonder how Stendhal would have felt about *this*," whispered Manja.

"We've explained who we are," I said. "What about you?"

"We're simply trying to get a good deal for taxpayers," a woman said. Then there was a knock, and she opened the door, clearly expecting someone. In came Stevo in a purple crushed velvet suit. I watched Manja try to suppress a sneer as he sat next to us.

"Here is our artist," said the chair. "Can you tell us how you began your career?"

"I went to the Royal College of Art with a student loan and graduated in 2010. Since then I've worked and networked in my spare time. Once I started getting press coverage, I met some more curators and now it's going alright."

"Did you ever need subsidies?"

"No, I used my programming skills to make the work and paid for the digital cameras myself."

"Where did you get those skills?" yelled Manja. "Who are your parents? Who did they know? How could you afford to live in London?"

"It's not fair to suggest that our friend hasn't worked extremely hard," said the chair as Stevo fumed at Manja. "You needn't get so angry, as the government, it turns out, agrees with you. We're just trying to persuade them that there are other options."

"I agree," said Claude.

"What?" replied Manja.

"I can make a living from selling things," Claude declared, grabbing a bottle of wine.

"This is our point," said one of the men.

"You started taking naked self-portraits because no-one bought your sculptures," said Manja. "And you're barely making anything from that."

"At least I'm not living off hand-outs!" replied Claude.

"Perhaps not," I said, "but who funds the galleries where you exhibit or the magazines that cover you?"

"They could crowdfund, or be supported by patrons," said the chair. "The common man shouldn't have to pay for works that he doesn't like."

"What the fuck do you know about the common man?" I shouted.

"Would you please leave," said the chair.

The same woman got up to open the door. I heard footsteps.

"Quick," she said, "the waiter's coming!"

As the women hurried to put flowers in their hair, the chair went to the laptop beneath the projector, closed Excel and put on a backdrop of green hills and a blue sky. Several men applied lipstick and mascara, and music started, which I recognised as *Wham*'s 'Club Tropicana'. They all sat, poured champagne and clinked their glasses as the food arrived.

Manja and I went to leave. She tapped Claude on the shoulder; Claude held up a glass of Bolly and we walked down the stairs without her. I returned the jacket to the cloakroom as we got our bags and wandered towards the bus stop.

"Did you see that piece that was around after we found out about David Cameron fucking that dead pig to get into that sex club at Oxford?" I asked.

"No," replied Manja.

"He just says that whenever he read about how lavish the Piers Gaveston Society parties were, he just remembered seeing loads of toffs with mullets and women in taffeta from C&A."

"What's C&A?" asked Manja, laughing.

"Cheap clothes shop," I said as the bus pulled up.

We turned to see Claude coming out of the club.

"I thought you were staying?" asked Manja.

"As soon as the waiter left, they went back to talking about benefit cuts," Claude replied.

"I'm sure they'll talk about their two minutes of decadence for years," I said, with a smile.

As Manja and I walked back towards Piccadilly Circus to get the 38 bus, I told her how I'd spent years trying to suss out how to complete 'Frankie Goes to Hollywood'. When I finally got through to the Pleasuredome, I just got a screen saying 'Welcome' with a bit of music. We changed at Dalston Junction, wondering how long it would be before the bars and clubs that we'd long loved here got replaced by ones that felt like Annabel's. Finally, we got home, unlocked the door and fell into bed together, not for a moment wishing we'd stayed for Stevo's after-party.

SERTRALINE SURREALISM

(AFTER CLAUDE CAHUN)

I read somewhere that the Romantic poets ate rotten meat before they went to sleep so that they would have more intense dreams. I can't remember where – I'm always memorising facts and quotes, but never where I saw them. It might have been in that Hugh Sykes Davies essay, 'Surrealism at This Time and Place', where he argues that Surrealism, rather than being a bold new movement – or even a fusion of Dada, Freudian psychoanalysis and revolutionary Marxism – was actually a continuation of Shelley, Byron, Coleridge and company, rendering it traditional and domestic, but probably not.

It doesn't matter: I have Sertraline.

'Abnormal dreams' are listed as an 'uncommon [side] effect': 0.1-1% of users experience them, but I am in that minority. I tried everything to manage my depression – radical politics, psychotherapy, gender reassignment, reading and writing – but nothing shifted it. Aged 34, with my first book – a memoir, which brought catharsis, but also plenty of worries about how to represent myself and the 'transgender community' – behind me, I felt I had no option besides SSRIs.

The effect that it would have on me would be revealed within a few weeks. Things that once induced panic now seemed manageable; the futility of life now felt like something I could address creatively, rather than meet with despair. For years, I worried that my mental health issues and artistic impulses were intrinsically linked – a precept fuelled by reading the Romantics with their fixation upon the neglected genius, as well as Breton's 'Nadja', René Crevel and other Surrealists, with their celebration of convulsive beauty. But not Claude Cahun: I didn't hear your name, or that of any Surrealist women who shaped their own worlds, until much later. My anxieties dissipated; I found it was easier to write with a clearer head. But as the drug kicked in, my frantic neural activity manifested itself in sleeping visions, which felt more real than anything in my waking life.

★

I'm outside L'Hôpital de la Pitié-Salpêtrière in the 13th arrondissement in Paris. After months of talking online, I'm meeting N. for the first time. N. translates the plaque on Jean-Martin Charcot's work on hypnosis and hysteria into a language that I understand; I take a moment to think about those women, and what might have driven them into such a condition, before we go into the garden. On a bench sits a blonde woman. A tarot reader shows her cards. I want to see them, but as I get close, the images turn into silver holograms. I request a reading but neither of them pay attention to me, and N. leads me inside the church.

I look for Charcot, but he cannot be found. Hysterical women line the pews, laughing spasmodically as N. and I walk up the aisle in matching outfits, white shirts with black ties and long, white, laced skirts with petticoats. As we reach the altar and pose for some photographs, they kneel. The statues of saints tell them to demand a cure – from N. and me. The congregation stand and march towards us: N. and I race through the park to a network of abandoned tunnels beneath the hospital. I read the graffiti – Front National *slogans and Anti-Fascist stickers* – *before we come out by a derelict building, its windows smashed.*

We enter through a red door with Joyeux Noël *daubed across it in white paint, and step into the corridor. We see Michelangelo's* 'Creation of Adam', *but God has breasts and a penis. S/he touches a naked woman* – 'Adam'? – *with hir fingertip. They are surrounded by faces that look familiar, but I don't recognise: maybe they are Artaud, Breton, Péret, Soupault et al. It is dated 3 October 1999, the day I turned eighteen, but it looks like the building was disused long before the end of the 20th century.* Didn't Claude Cahun write that 'the year 2000' would be 'the end of the world'? *I remember about the Millennium Bug, which passed without incident, and the apocalyptic events in New York, twenty-one months later, and all that came after.*

Next, we see two dining rooms. The one on the left is painted white, the walls bare, its windows barred: this must have been for the patients. The right-hand room is mustard yellow, with Klimt and Courbet on display, the window looking at the park and the hospital in the distance. Both rooms are set up for Christmas dinner, with fine china and cutlery on pristine tablecloths, with crackers and tinsel, but there is nobody in sight.

Unnerved, we return to the corridor. The mural has vanished. Only the date remains: 18 July 2012, the day of my sex reassignment surgery. A stern man with white hair and thick eyebrows grabs me. You do not fit, *he says.* Neuter is the only gender that always suits me, *I reply, before N. asks,* I thought you preferred 'she' and 'her'. *He lunges at N. I reach for N.'s hand and watch as my companion vanishes into thin air.* Your voice is male, *he insists.* How do you know? *He strips me, and then forces a needle into my left breast. As a group of men* – *medics or psychiatrists* – *rush through the door and drag me out, I wake up, sweating.*

★

ME: That dream. It's not real.

N: Of course it's not. The symbolism is too convenient.

ME: No, I mean, it actually happened.

N: Nonsense.

ME: You took me to the Salpêtrière and told me about Charcot. It was a dream-like experience, sure, but we did go to the hospital and the church, and through those tunnels to that abandoned building.

N: Maybe so, but I'm a composite of several of your friends, you've changed lots of the details and none of those other people were there.

ME: Perhaps I dreamt them.

N: No, you wrote them.

ME: What is writing, if not lucid dreaming?

N: But when you write, you're in complete control.

ME: It's true that I create characters and put them in situations, often drawing on 'real life'... after that, I never know what'll happen. If I did, I'd have no interest in writing it. Sometimes they do things I don't expect, or even that I find abhorrent. It's not quite the same as a normal dream where you're a spectator in a scenario that your subconscious throws at you, I admit. Years ago, I had a period of lucid dreaming. They never lasted long, maybe just a few seconds. But at some point, I'd know I was in a dream, and could make decisions. If it was a nightmare, I could make myself wake up.

N: Did you keep a diary of them?

ME: Only occasionally. I felt that writing them down would change them. I might misremember or embellish them, or even influence them in advance.

N: Did you enjoy them?

ME: Yes – my job at the time was unbearably dull, so it was the best form of escapism.

★

I was always bored easily, even as a child – especially as a child – trying to make mundane suburbia more captivating. Anything that created its own world interested me: video games; music; movies; novels. All that I consumed formed sediment in my mind, and it became impossible to tell what settled and what evaporated. I knew that Dada and Surrealism, Futurism, transgender theory and lived experience were important to me, whilst Romanticism, rationalism and religion were not – but none of them transformed my waking hours into anything transcendent, or raised my dreams above reflections of my anxiety and frustration.

Gradually, I realised that being a neglected artist or a convulsive beauty was not what I'd been sold. The numerous rejections may not have been because I was ahead of my time, but because I wasn't good enough; being desirable to men attracted to transgender women usually resulted in objectification, or molestation. Before I turned thirty, it had worn me down so much that I asked my GP for anti-depressants, and left with a prescription of 20mg of Citalopram per day.

The suicidal thoughts lifted, as did the initial headaches and nausea. I lost my appetite and often felt exhausted, but was terrified of sleeping as I had such awful nightmares. Old friends who I'd alienated with my refusal to tolerate anything I thought mediocre, returning to reproach me... Victorian ailments... hysteria... elephantiasis... public humiliation at the hands of a mistress... On waking, I reoriented myself, but when sleeping, lines between dream and reality became indistinguishable. This, however, was not what I'd intended. I came off the medication, my appetite returned, I had more energy and my dreams calmed down. I decided to try again to manage my depression through my material world – but eventually the cycle turned me back to the pharmaceutical. This time, maybe, the side effects have been manageable – or perhaps, five years older, I'm willing to accept more of them if there is an overall improvement.

★

Staying sane is a lifetime's work.

★

I knew your name, Claude, but hadn't read *Disavowals* (or: 'Cancelled Confessions') when I was documenting my gender reassignment (first for a newspaper, then as a memoir). If I had, maybe I would have seen parallels between your declaration that 'neuter is the only gender that always suits me' and my conclusion that 'there are as many gender identities as there are people; all unique, all constantly being explored in conscious and unconscious ways'. My articles were fragments, although they had to be realist, transparent like a windowpane, written against myself and the literature I loved. Appropriately, it seems, your work came to me in pieces, an oblique self-portrait in a *Queer Art and Culture* volume here, a taster of Sarah Pucill's film *Magic Mirror*, which turned passages and images from *Disavowals* into tableaux, there.

I finally encountered your work in its fractured whole when a friend from Jersey who identified with your subversion of the island's Nazi occupation curated an exhibition of your photos with *Magic Mirror* and asked me to speak about your writing. It was hard to gather my thoughts on something so disparate: I admired that you could write *for yourself* and not bend your style into something sellable (even if your literary family background gave you all the intellectual and financial support that one could ever need). But what of that book that you assembled over nearly a decade, and finally published in May 1930, in an edition of five hundred copies, that wasn't translated into English until 2007 – long after the point in my life when I most needed it?

I found ten sections, fronted by photo-collages that reminded me of Hannah Höch, a mixture of self-portraits, familiar-looking faces (Breton and his friends?), discon-nected bits of women's bodies, and my favourite, the chess board under an ominous shadow that reminded me of Dada, Duchamp, *Sélavy*. Most of them were titled with acronyms, private jokes decipherable only to you, but one stood out: 'Myself (For want of anything better)'.

Then, instantly, you turned towards and away from yourself, cloaking yourself in metaphorical prose-poetry, opting out of that autobiographical pact by giving 'False impressions', before asking: 'Express oneself: humiliate oneself? Yes, but for the right reason.' But what *are* the right reasons? Is it the Narcissism, the 'Non-co-operation with God' and 'passive resistance' that you wrote about so nakedly, Lacanian before Lacan; the need to record one's existence, or subjectivity, before leaving the stage? Was it a realisation that 'the personal is political' *avant la lettre*, and that documenting your games with gender and identity might inspire others to make themselves into works of art? Or was it just that there was so much pain, in being Jewish, (assigned) female, and queer in an anti-Semitic, misogynist and homophobic world that you had to get these words out, and throw them at *someone*, even if (as you knew) it wouldn't be many people, at least not in your lifetime?

'Trample on this, this flesh of my flesh. Draw on remorse, weigh on my memory, on my obese statue, the only springboard that doesn't give way under me.' This sentence: I understood why you would cancel your confessions, the nightmare of being in a position where readers, critics, editors demand that you give more away to keep them coming back, the hope that external validation might fix your sense of self, stop it receding ever further. They will define you, and then you won't know who or where you are. Nonetheless – I don't regret putting my life on a page, and I don't get the sense that you did either.

★

Even if you weren't quite a part of the Surrealist group that so intrigued me – and given how hostile they were to anything besides heterosexuality, and how women were rarely more than obscure objects of desire for them I can understand why – your writing and self-portraits felt so phantasmagorical, and so resonant, that I hoped we might meet in the very eye of night.

I'm back at school, in Surrey. I have this dream all the time, and it's always unbearable. I don't want to be here, and I don't need to do my GCSEs again. Nonetheless, I walk through the gate, past the bike shed and the basketball court, past the playground where I spent every lunchtime kicking a tennis ball around in my itchy trousers. I stare up at the five-storey tower block and then wonder why I keep coming here when I could just bunk the train to Brighton and...

I enter by the English rooms and go past the library. There is a sign: ARTISTS' SALON. *Anyone seen there* **will** *get their heads kicked in, I think, and then decide that I'm sick of having my life choices dictated by a small gang of bullies, and nervously enter.*

Behind the door, there is a beach. It is night-time. I look up at the stars, and then at two men climbing into sailboats. The boat on the left has no name; the one on the right, smaller, has an inscription reading 'Ocean Wave'. *They set off – I wade into the water to try to stop them, but a voice stops me, telling me to let them complete their own legends. I turn: a person is sat alone, a chequered shirt and a shaved head. As I sit and watch the men drift over the horizon, oblivious to each other, the sea turns into a mirror, and we stare at our reflections – neither of us recognisably male nor female.*

CLAUDE: Hi, I'm Claude. I'm your Careers Officer. Nice to meet you. *[Silence.]* What do you want to do after you leave school?
ME: Become a woman.
CLAUDE: No – I mean for work.
ME: I don't know... Well, I want to be a writer. Everyone keeps telling me to forget it.
CLAUDE: I write. I just don't obsess about becoming famous for it.
ME: Lucky you.
CLAUDE: You said you wanted to become a woman. Write about that.
ME: I'm not sure.

Claude pulls out some tarot cards. I imagine that these will confirm whether or not I will reach my goal, but once again, I cannot see what is printed on them. Claude grins, and returns them to a shirt pocket. I look at Claude, frustrated.

CLAUDE: It would be boring to write about something if you knew what was going to happen. *(I shrug.)* The destination never matters – it's the journey. Write about the clothes you wear, the labels you give yourself, and the sex you have with people of many genders, or no gender. Your mutilated victories and your brave defeats. The dreams you have and the body you inhabit in them. Write because you want to, and because you have to, not because of what you think it might bring to you. And only show it to people if you think it will liberate them. Or you.

I nod, and leave the room. I step outside, and the school has turned into the hospital where I worked as a cleaner when I was 16. The wards are named after towns and villages in Surrey: Ashtead, Earlswood, Horley. I walk along the sterile corridors, listening to the sounds of women screaming from the single rooms – doctors pull the curtains as I pass.

I go back outside. Instead of the playground and basketball court are lakes, and the tower block has been replaced by a grandiose Victorian building, redbrick with large windows and pillars, with a perfectly ordered garden leading up to it. I walk along the path to enter, and see Claude, sat in the waiting room. As I reach the reception, a surgeon takes me into a laboratory, and injects me with anaesthetic. At the moment I fall asleep, I wake up.

★

That wasn't a real dream either. Nor, of course, was it reality. The symbolism is too convenient, too obviously an encounter that I'd have liked to have had, when I had no possibility models (Laverne Cox's phrase, which I prefer to 'role models') in life or in literature. If it was a dream, I doubt the dialogue would have been that clear, or that memorable – normally, I can only recollect fragments of conversations held in my dreams, and those who have shared a room or a bed with me in this state tell me that I either mumble something incomprehensible, or utter just a couple of distinct words, usually ones that embarrass me.

My Sertraline dreams far outstrip normality, as I am a spectator to long conversations that play out with friends and acquaintances, heroes and villains, the living and the dead. These must happen during my deepest sleep: a friend says that lucid dreams are a stage between that and waking, but these visions elude my control. I sometimes wonder what Charcot would have made of them; I hope that Cahun would have told me to embrace them, and draw upon them by day and night. Even when they're nightmarish, I could tell Claude, I want to turn them into poetry and prose, as a weapon against reality, or what I am constantly told to accept as 'reality' – usually by those who have the most invested in upholding the world as it is.

ONE HUNDRED
YEARS AGO

One Sunday afternoon, whilst I was lying on my bed reading a novel, my father returned from a trip down the A23, having paid a visit to his mother's house with its fraying, browning wallpaper, carrying a cardboard box of photographs. *I thought you might be interested in these,* he said, bringing them to my room. I thanked him and spread the pictures out across my old mahogany desk, itself a hand-me-down from a distant, departed relative – one of my mother's uncles, who I never met. Amongst the snapshots of my father with my mother, his mother, and his sister, and of various weddings, which had the same musty smell that I associated with my grandmother's living room, were a handful of my great-aunt Elsie – the first family member who I can recall dying, when I was six and she was ninety-one, and the only one not to move to the suburbs after the Second World War.

My grandparents were Londoners: first Kensington, where they met through a mutual friend; then Paddington, after my great-grandfather somehow survived Passchendaele; and finally, Tooting. My grandmother wanted children as soon as they got married, but her husband was called up a few weeks after their honeymoon. She was too old to be evacuated – instead, the day after the Balham Tube disaster, she decided to flee. Not wanting to go too far, so she bought a terraced house in Surrey, even though Croydon got hit with more Doodlebugs than anywhere else because they fell short of the capital. A few years after VE Day, they started a family. My father went to Wallington County Grammar, his sister to Carshalton High, and neither dreamt of returning to the capital with its bombed-out buildings, its prefabricated towers and estates, its Victorian resonances, areas designated as *vicious, semi-criminal* or, if they were lucky, *chronic want*. Indeed, my father moved further down the London-Brighton line, to its midway point, too far from either for me to find a night life, a cultural life, much life at all.

Aunt Elsie had long fascinated me because she was always discussed in sombre tones. The phrase *never married* cropped up in every conversation about her, but nobody ever elaborated. The question of whether she'd ever found someone she wanted to marry was never asked, let alone if not wanting to marry was a valid choice.

The first photograph was a sepia portrait in a cardboard frame, clearly posed. My father said the family had not yet owned a camera when it was taken – Kodak made popular photography possible only a few years earlier with their Brownie box camera and cheap film; the first images taken at home dated from the early 1920s. It had 'American Studios, (The Boston)' printed on the bottom-left, and '29, High St, Kensington, W.' on the bottom-right. The photo – helpfully labelled with 'Eleanor Joy Gartside', ('auntie Elsie'), date of birth (12.4.1896), 'about 10 yrs old?' and '6" x4"' in the top-left – peered through an oval cutting, surrounded by a garland resembling a daisy chain, printed but designed to look hand-drawn.

The picture had a two-tone background; the lighter parts looked like clouds, making it feel even more haunting, or haunted. I couldn't tell if this was down to the early 20th century technology, or if the photographer had used a screen. Elsie's deep eyes (blue-green or hazel, the tint made it hard to tell) and dense but perfectly groomed eyebrows focused on the lens; her thin, pursed lips had a melancholy look but betrayed little emotion, while the shadow on the left of her face somehow emphasised the distance between her and her family, her and her time, her time and mine. I envied her hair: dark, wavy, secured on each side by a hairpin, falling past her shoulders, settling on the lace of her gingham dress with its chokingly high neckline.

The most striking aspect, however, was the doll on her lap. It was made of fine china, a bonnet on its head and a ribbon round its chin, with tiny, painted lips, its expression as curious as Elsie's was cautious. Its dress was like its owner's; its little hands seemed to be grasping at Elsie's, as if they each knew that the other was the only presence in the world they could trust.

There was another image that, whilst not carrying the same strangely reassuring odour of the oldest one, visibly complemented it – I wasn't sure if this was intentional. Printed on Kodak paper, with a shiny finish that caught the light, it was marked 'Elsie and Gertie, 3 May 1976' in my grandmother's writing. It caught Elsie in her early eighties, still more than ten years from death, concentrating on the camera. It was in a size that had become standard by then, and the earliest taken in colour, but her eyes were too shrunken behind her glasses to determine their shade, and her hair – cropped short – was mostly white. The Edwardian frock had been replaced by a simple, button-up blouse, the doll by a tabby cat, happy to settle on her lap. Elsie looked even less comfortable being photographed than she had in her childhood, and despite her companion, somehow lonelier: I wondered if she was thinking about her doll. Maybe it had been lost or broken, or perhaps she gave it to my grandmother in the absence of any children of her own.

I began to speculate about what her life might have been like throughout those seven decades. I wondered if she *never married* because her sweetheart was slaughtered on the Western Front, and the heartbreak never lifted. However, my mother often talked about her great-uncle, who died at the Somme, and if Elsie had lost a lover in the same conflict, then surely I would have known. Maybe she had relationships with men but was never able, or *never wanted* to settle down. She had stayed in the metropolis after all, rather than evacuating herself to some soulless satellite town, neighbours gardening on Saturday, gossiping on Sunday, longing for death in a loveless marriage. But if she *had* tried to find a suitor, somebody in my family would have expressed regret that none of them turned out to be The One: a minor tragedy that would have at least dared to speak its name.

I stared at a postcard of Elsie at Portobello Road School, '13 or 14 years', and wondered if, for her, the classroom had become a place full of lust. Most of the girls wore gymslips over white blouses, but Elsie, for some reason was all in black. If I had been asked to guess where the image was from, I doubt I would have said Britain: there was a similarity to their hairstyles, and a seriousness to their expressions, that I might have identified as German before I realised that it was difference in time rather than place that accounted for its unfamiliarity. To my surprise, Elsie came the closest to a smile of the twenty-eight in her class, although it seemed more a look of contentment than happiness. I could spend hours thinking about who they all were, where they lived, who they loved and when they died, whether they worked and what they did, and how I might find out. Maybe the girl at the back, whose face had faded more than anyone else, heightening the tentative fear in her upturned eyes, had died young, of some illness easily treated now but not before the advent of penicillin. Perhaps she'd been killed by the V2s, or even the 'baby-killer' Zeppelins. Perhaps another had colonial links, even a mixed parentage that could never be discussed, and left this country to become an administrator, a tiny cog in an oppressive Empire, deliberately kept ignorant of its multiple atrocities.

I wondered how many of them Elsie considered friends, or confided in. If she thought being attracted to a girl made her a Sapphist, or an invert, or a lesbian, although I doubt if she knew any of those terms. Maybe she conceived of this as something she felt, rather than something she *was*, yearning for a day when it might be easier to discuss, or if she told herself that these inclinations were purely because there were no boys in her class, and once she was older, she would feel like *normal women*. What if she had a furtive fling with one of the girls, maybe the one in the fourth row with short hair and no gymslip, meeting away from their claustrophobic terraces, avoiding each other's glances in whatever lessons the school deigned to teach to girls. Then their worries about what might happen if anyone else found out, their knowledge that there was little point in thinking beyond their next clandestine encounter, which made sure it was over before it had ever really begun.

Elsie would have had to wait until she had left school, and home, to have any kind of relationship. How would she have paid for her own place? By moving East or South, to one of London's poorer districts, where a sense of space, let alone sanctuary, would have been unattainable? She couldn't have lived with a woman there, realistically, but she could have moved closer to someone. I guessed she spent many nights at home, wherever that was; sometimes with a partner, whom she could never introduce to her family, but most often alone, her hand reaching across to an empty space where a partner was supposed to lie. On a good night, her cat might have filled the void, settling down as she stroked it, purring as she fell asleep to mitigate the loneliness.

No: I wanted to imagine Elsie finding a way to be happy, at least within her limits. The end of the war – the first one – might have opened a world for her. Women could vote, work in new fields, and afford their own homes. They could spend time together with no men around. I don't know how Elsie might have connected with someone, whether she was open about her feelings soon after meeting a woman she liked, or whether it was an agonising process of being introduced to someone and trying to communicate through various innuendos, that either marked her as a sharer of a secret, or just as irredeemably strange. But there was no cottaging for women, no Polari, and I have no idea which signs she could have used.

Either way, she would have made her home feel like a refuge, maybe on the ground floor so people in her block were less likely to see the same woman leaving several mornings a week, so she wouldn't have to climb numerous stairs when she popped in to feed the cat on the way to her girlfriend's place, doing enough to secure its love during those times when she had to be solitary.

How sad that a relationship should be so confined – but less sad than never being able to love at all. It wasn't impossible, after all: plenty of accounts of the inter-war period discuss women who built a life together. But they were always independently wealthy, in a way that Elsie just wasn't. Those couples could grow because they *had* friends and confidantes, in open-minded cultural circles, who would support them in public; their writing helped them to build networks. I don't know what Elsie did for a living; I doubt if my family would appreciate my speculation, even though I do so sympathetically. I don't feel able to ask many questions. Her love life must have joined my great-grandfather's war injury — a respiratory condition induced by mustard gas — in the pantheon of things never to be discussed, harrowing memories only unleashed after their funerals.

She would have still had the same problem, then, as at school — the main difference being that she would probably have been able to find *some* supportive people, and wouldn't have felt so trapped, at least not in quite the same way. Would she have confided in my grandmother? I don't think so: not unless the prospect of her niece letting slip and the consequent awkwardness (at best) didn't bother her. She would have talked with her lover(s), obviously, but more in terms of strategies to avoid detection. If she had problems with a relationship — where could she vent? A diary, if found, could break apart a shared life, and anything long-term would smash against the rock of not feeling able to live together.

I closed my eyes and willed Elsie's ghost into my room. No, that was stupid; I tried to imagine the conversation we could have, spanning each end of our century, where she told me what things were like for women like her and I explained how they are for women like me. (Even if, I imagined, she might not believe me.) Perhaps I would tell her how things would get better, if not for her, then for her kind: there would be lesbian politicians and film stars, magazines and novels; women could look for a home together without being disowned; you might be able to tell people at work (if not school) and the sky would not cave in. To my surprise, Elsie told me that, going from her experience, things would improve for me, too. It *would* become easier to find empathetic confidantes, especially if people had become as confident as I suggested, and — she said with her enigmatic half-smile that I doubted if she'd used since sitting at her desk at the Portobello Road School – sometimes you have low expectations of someone, and maybe that's best, but they pleasantly surprise you. I opened my eyes and Elsie spirited herself away, back into the photograph of the haunted-looking child, clutching her doll for dear life, and I put the box into the wardrobe next to my bed, taking solace in the awareness that what had passed between us could remain secret from my family.

A REPORT ON THE I-SMILE HAPPINESS WATCH

A REPORT ON THE
i-Smile Happiness smart watch
Rebecca Pennock, BA (Hons), MA

Abstract

The i-Smile smart watch has recently been developed to measure personal happiness using a number of kinetic metrics. In this experiment, I decided to test the watch on its own merits, using its percentage points both as a guide to my own behaviour, and an indication of its programmers' ideas of what constitutes emotional well-being.

Introduction

Gridlocked traffic, summer solstice, 9.15am. Upper deck 243, Dalston Junction to Goswell Road, who wouldn't look down on this sort of commute? I'm sure I did, scarf in June, four homeless people asking for help by the luxury flats that now line Kingsland Road, newspaper boards about NHS failures, twee little cafés where there used to be gig venues, supermarkets built over social services, mobile phone shouting that distracts you from reading. We turned before Bishopsgate and its *Blade Runner* nightmare: Old Street roundabout, JC Decaux and Google and their LCD future, some Android gadget that will cure my depression, keep me on time, in touch with my friends, in tune with the world…

We weren't going to move so I decided to walk. My umbrella broke but the rain hit me sideways so it would've been useless. Ten minutes later, half an hour late, I got to reception. Big screen, Sky News, hundreds of migrants drown in the Med then in/terminable fights in the two major parties, Corbyn's too left-wing, Cameron's too left-wing. Swiped in, ground floor, pressed the button for the fourth, dripping wet, harsh rigid lines of this open plan nightmare. I never signed up for this. *Yes you did,* says Maria, *we all did.* I didn't mean the job itself, I meant the- 231 emails / no time / morning briefing / Christ.

Sit at the back, sketchbook out. A man and a flipchart, I don't know the face but I know that haircut, it must come with those suits. OHP: external consultant, he means business, lives it, breathes it. His mundanity moves me, so I note what he says:

– *We're thrilled to be partnering you on this new project. Content/ment Solutions have been working on the i-Smile Watch for three years, and because your manager said you were all interested in digital technology, we thought you'd like to help us develop it.*

He went round the room, handing all twelve of us an expensive piece of kit. A few people wore it immediately, pleased at the thought of their emotions becoming Big Data. Others examined it. No Off switch, apparently.

The i-Smile watch, as you might guess [he laughs, forced] *measures worker happiness. Not from what you say, like in your one-to-ones, but kinetically, from what you* do *– how you move, your tone of voice, what energy you carry around. It will give feedback on how relaxed or uptight you are, which emotions you transmit* *through your speech patterns, which people you meet with kindness and which with hostility. It's our hope that the device will understand these better than you, providing some constructive feedback, and help you to manage your workplace relationships better.*

I leant back in my chair, waiting for the revolt. None. *Nothing to hide, nothing to fear.*

Any questions?

– What will this info be used for?

– *Simply to help your management make your office a happier environment.*

– How long do we have to wear these?

– *The experiment lasts a month. We ask that you wear these at work for the whole period – if you want to record or submit data in your own time, that's up to you. It'd be a big help.*

He gave me the watch, stood over me as I put it on. *Smile!* We both knew that what I did was a grimace, and I went back to my desk.

Methods

I took off the watch and put it away. I peered at Maria, struggling to make hers comfortable. CPUs humming, fans whirring, birds outside singing. Rich swaggered past, shit-eating grin: *Not wearing yer watch Becs?* I shook my head. *Cheer up love it might never 'appen.* He's like that prick at those parties, late 1990s, I'd chat in the corner and he would berate me: *Have fun! That's not* fun*!*

Half an hour later, Maria leant over.

– *I don't know why,* she said, *but just wearing this makes me feel better.* I had nothing to say. *Maybe it's because I know it* will *make me happier.*

– *Or maybe you don't want anyone to know that you're miserable,* I replied.

– *Maybe you don't want to know that* you're *miserable,* she told me, and I didn't think she was joking.

But I *am* miserable, and don't see why I should hide it: so why do those rebukes hurt so much? The woman in halls who asked, "Why do you hate the world?" when I knew full well that I *did* hate the world, or at least how it's run, but it made me feel awful...

   — *You're not even going to wear yours, are you?*

   — *I don't know. I'm not in the mood.*

She half-laughed and went back to her work.

From: Rebecca.pennock@thecompany.org
To: Senior.Manager@thecompany.org
Subject: Meeting

Hi,

Can we talk in private?

Rebecca

Rebecca Pennock
Customer Service Advisor

Glass-box meeting room. Everyone can see who you're talking to... your gestures... expressions... when you start crying...

   — *Can't I opt out of this?*

   — *But you're one of the people I was most worried about. Every day I see you, shoulders dropped, head down, not talking. Wouldn't you be happier in a happier place?*

   — *Well of course, but how can I live in London and make art without a job?*

   — *I didn't mean that, I meant that you'd be happier if we made a nicer environment.*

   — *I guess...*

— *If you still can't find any positivity, you're free to look elsewhere…*

— *What's the point?*

I shrugged and put on the watch. Maybe it could become a project. I'd have to be like the consultant: live happiness, breathe happiness, *dream* happiness. *Did that mean getting* inside *his head?* Perhaps if I dressed differently…

Charity shop, Kingsland Road, new gear for work. Pinstripe suit? Power-dressing *c.*1985, I'm not Theresa fucking May, those people try to look more casual now, or more restrained. Black heels so I don't slouch – jacket – knee-length skirt, navy blue like I'm back at school – *happiest days of your life.*

7.30 alarm, starting score of 20% – must have been the groans as I stopped hitting snooze. Brisk shower, tried not to get annoyed at the state of the bath or my flatmate never cleaning the sink. Left home, head up, headphones off to embrace the world. *Smile at those who smile at me, talk to those who talk to me…*

Sunny so I walked to work. I hit 45%, getting exercise and vitamin D, all the things the doctor orders… Shoreditch High Street, infantilised nightmare, signs saying 'It's a hot shop for cool people… Lolz!' or 'War is peace / Freedom is slavery / Ignorance is strength / Time for tea', *austalgia* for those who believed that the Tories after the Credit Crunch were the same as Labour after the Second World War…

You can't think like that, the watch reminds me, showing 32%. The Boxpark doesn't help, that apparently temporary 'pop-up' mall with shops in hangars, its aesthetic stolen from the early 2000s clubs where I strove for happiness with MDMA. I think about that cat café and that cereal bar for London's ever-expanding kidult population and then reach Great Eastern St. I turn off before that heart-warming graffiti, 'Snowden, E.', the comma most likely added after the writer spelled the surname wrong, thumbing its nose at the vanity towers and the surveillance industry, and the thought puts me 2% up before I pass Hoxton 7 with its 'happy hour' that lasts from 12 to 8.30.

There's an advert for more flats that won't help the housing crisis, SE1, this time called *The Music Box* – I hate that they've named it after Laurel & Hardy but it's less offensive than 'Avant-Garde Towers' off Bethnal Green Road, where I bet the first thing the residents do is get the experimental cinema shut down...

The Shoreditch Art Wall just has a badly painted Corona advert, opposite the slogan for the Village Underground club, 'Let's adore and endure each other'. There's *Child of the Jago* too, a stylish clothes shop named after a novel about Victorian poverty in this part of London, poor and undesirable ever since the people of the City threw their shit over the walls. I move down a few percent as I walk up towards Old Street station, and it strikes me that for all the people who ask for money on Kingsland Road, there isn't anyone sat in the subways like there always was: they haven't put spikes on the floor like in West London, but maybe the Council decided that the homeless don't fit the new Old Street vibe, all pop-up street-food, pop music, fake art and coffee shops, all the hallmarks of that East London, anti-corporate search for authenticity turned into entrepreneurial opportunity, and moved them somewhere sadder.

The imperative to happiness, rather than the removal of signs of imperfection, featured mainly in advertising, trying to hide the way that the possibility of *every* space being bought makes public life feel grubby and empty. My watch never scored higher than 45%, and only wavered above 35% when I saw ads for music I like – Autechre, Aphex Twin – and thought it might mean someone else feeling like I did when I first heard '*Flutter*' or '*Raising the Titanic*', and then felt depressed that those sounds had been commodified like everything else.

I noted one other thing, as I approached the office. I looked over at St Luke's Parochial School and its declaration that it was founded in 1698, and then up the street at a building where an old Salvation Army inscription remained. The prosaic temperance of a Protestant past had been replaced: where the hoardings outside St Luke's Education Centre would once have read 'Closed for refurbishment' or 'Under construction', they now yell: 'Having a makeover!'

Everything has to be *fun*. What happens if we stop enjoying ourselves, for even a moment?

★

I stood outside, deep breaths. *That's for anxiety,* I thought, and tried to recall moments of happiness. Barely any movement, 33-34%, a sharp drop as soon as the office came into view. *Positive attitude,* I told myself – I smiled at the temp on reception, at the digital start-up people from other floors, and registered a slight rise on my wrist, even though I didn't believe my own projection. Still, I got in on time and got straight into my work.

– *You're early,* I heard from across the desk.

– *Bright on time,* I replied.

– *Are you alright?*

I just grinned. Surprise flashed across Maria's eyes but, to her credit, she returned my smile. As I wondered if we understood each other a little better, I watched the number on my watch spike, just momentarily, until I caught her gaze again and saw that sarcastic look that insisted: *This won't last.*

I opened my emails. *Subject: Customer Service Training.* 'I'll do that', I wrote, picking a date after consulting my diary.

Three mornings later, an appointment flashed up on Excel. I went back into a glass box: my manager sat there with his iPad, a soft, welcoming look on his face that I hadn't seen since he told me *You've got the job.*

— *It's only been a few days but I've really noticed a change, it's like you've become a different person.* Pause: *Is it the watch?*

— *My scores were very low…* He tilts his head, sympathetically, as if to say *I'm not surprised. So I thought that if I tried to get on with people, get involved with things…*

— *We'll have to start an Employee of the Month award for you,* he replies. Low laughter. I couldn't stop myself smiling. He smiled back; I thought I could *feel* a movement on my wrist, *absurd, it can't put out endorphins…* He told me to go to the training room in the afternoon, and to enjoy myself, and fleetingly, I wondered if I might.

I got there on time. Just a couple of others, who seemed nice enough. They stared at their phones, so I joined them. For once, finding nothing new felt like a reason for calm, not anxiety: I put it away, logged in, sat and waited. But I could tell who was taking the training from the way the door swung open.

— *Hi everyone, I'm Rich — I'm taking training today as Jen is off sick and — Rebecca Peacock! Never thought I'd see you here!*

— *Well, you have,* I said, trying to smile. He raised his eyebrows and checked his notes, and I knew that however much I tried to make this more tolerable, he would try to force me back into the miser role that he had created for me, and then defined himself against. I spent the next two hours trying to ignore his smug little grins, ironic-unironic remarks about how I'd end up running the place, his passive-aggressive platitudes about life being what you make it, and how stupid it was to ever consider 'Artist' a "realistic career choice". I watched the percentage plummet to its lowest yet, and hadn't even learned anything about customer service.

Results

I was doing everything right and everything wrong. I got back to my desk to find that already, Maria was passing phone enquiries to me; when the first caller ranted about a problem with a driver for our 3D modelling software, I said nothing until he started yelling, then put down the receiver and set the handset to Mute. I spent the rest of the day on the internet, in the canteen, going to the shop, anything as long it wasn't my caseload of press contacts, complaints for the Technical Team, or anything else that the computer could do, quite happily, without me.

I was surprised that I got away with this for nearly a week before the manager took me aside.

– Rebecca, you were doing so well. What happened? I shrugged, unable to say that something inside me had broken, as far as my ability to stomach this job was concerned, and couldn't be fixed. Unable to say that I didn't understand how so many people around me didn't feel the same: they must have left for university with the same ambitions and dreams as me, the same promises made by those in power, the same belief that if they kept listening and reading and thinking and engaging, then life would somehow reward them…

I gave the watch to him. He raised his eyes – I'd not checked the score for days, but it must have been low enough for him to understand that it'd be better if I left. He didn't stop me: I passed through the gates, put my pass on the Security desk and stepped out, wondering what to do now, resisting the urge to go back and apologise, knowing that struggling by on the dole would make me happier than this.

Discussion

In my spare time, I re-read Alenka Zupančič's book *The Odd One In: On Comedy,* where she writes that 'In the contemporary ideological climate it has become imperative that we perceive all the terrible things that happen to us as ultimately something positive' – in my case, turning the hated surveillance into an art piece, something that I performed and would continue to perform, was just that: a protective measure against the minor injuries and humiliations of the world of work. 'Negativity, lack, dissatisfaction, unhappiness, are perceived more and more as moral faults – worse, as a corruption at the level of our very being'. This 'bio-morality', she states, 'promotes the fundamental axiom: a person who feels good (and is happy) is a good person: a person who feels bad is a bad person... This is very efficient, for who dares to raise her voice and say that she is not happy, and can't manage to – or worse, doesn't even care to – transform all the disappointments of her life into a positive experience'?

Paradoxically, it was only by making this statement that I made myself feel any better – and I'm sure that it did the opposite to my colleagues, who either had to replace me or take on my work, and had to reassess or repress their feelings about what they did, who they were. As I scanned various websites and local papers to fill out my Jobseekers' diary and get my £71 a week, I wondered if I could be happy in anything less than a socialist utopia – but even then, I thought, there would be no need for *art*, and then how would I fill my days?

A REVIEW OF *A RETURN*

REVIEW

Film Diary I: A Return (2020)

J. G. Singer's latest work is an ambiguous, ambivalent chronicle of the small, suburban town where the filmmaker grew up, and an intriguing look into who gets excluded from such places and why. However, it doesn't say as much as it could, even when it reveals more than it intended. Words by *Phil Hamilton*.

When *Syntagma* journal asked if I wanted to review J. G. Singer's new film – an hour-long walk through their hometown in Surrey, shot on 16mm with Singer's narration and an ambient soundtrack – I was hesitant. I've long been interested in Singer's work, not so much because I share Špela Milanič's conviction, expressed in her review of *Summer Days* (2018), that Singer is 'the most promising queer experimental filmmaker in contemporary Europe', but because I knew Singer in our youth. That would not be a problem in many instances – I would happily interview Singer (who uses they/them pronouns) or include their work in any survey of recent queer film. But a review presents an ethical consideration, demanding objectivity as it does. In this case, I think it more interesting, and potentially productive, to write *through* this moral issue than to recoil from it, hence my accepting this commission. I hope that you, the reader, will indulge me, and I hope J. G. Singer will forgive me.

With its title betraying the influence of great film diarists such as Jonas Mekas or David Perlov, *A Return* opens on a train. The image flickers and fades in, awakening the viewer somewhere between Earlswood and Salfords on the London-Brighton line. With that characteristic 16mm light burn around the edges of the shot, Singer shows us the Royal Earlswood Hospital, or the Asylum for Idiots as it was called when it opened in 1853 – the first purpose-built establishment for people with learning disabilities. "Who knows how many horrors took place in this fortress," reflects Singer, telling us about two cousins of the Queen who were hidden there and listed as dead in *Burke's Peerage,* decades before their actual deaths and burial, in one case, in the nearby Redstone cemetery. Described by architectural critic Ian Nairn simply as 'not nice', the listed building looms over the surrounding countryside, and now serves as luxury flats (of course) with a Union Jack flying over the top – a whitewashing of a complicated past that perhaps reveals more about *A Return* than Singer intended.

The film *really* begins when Singer gets off at Horley station, offers glimpses of the privatised train company logos and reminiscences about British Rail despite being too young to remember it. Unlike their early works about London, where Singer moved "as soon as I legally could" (to study at Goldsmiths, naturally), the narration does not strive too hard for the effect of Patrick Keiller, noting simply that "History never happens here." But there are personal histories, and people with histories, as *A Return* explores. The first of these is quite amusing: Singer sees a man sat in a car waiting outside the station, picking his nose, who they immediately recognise as "Mr Norton, who threatened to expel me in Year 10 because he thought I'd put glue in his coffee. I hadn't, but I think he'd just never liked me because he thought I was too girly, and a bit of a smart-arse." Then, a lament: "So did everyone else." At this point, the man in the car realises he's being filmed, and angrily turns towards the camera; the shot ends abruptly, most likely with Singer running away like a naughty schoolchild.

There are a few establishing shots to tell us more about what kind of town this is: a large Waitrose and an old but well-maintained department store; a sign for Horley Tyre & Exhaust (that may have inspired the pun that opens Shena Mackay's 1986 novel 'Redhill Rococo', set in the next town up, where the protagonist sees 'Redhill exhausts and tires' when getting off the train there); and the big Wetherspoon pub, in what was once "a grand cinema, back in the Thirties". (He's wrong about this: the cinema was demolished in 1981, and the Art Deco building used to be a car showroom, run by the family of local racing driver Jack Fairman, after whom the pub is named.) Then Singer takes us to the secondary school – the only one in the town – to poke at their memory further, having already set up an unhappy time there with that earlier anecdote. It's break-time: children are eating, talking, playing football or basketball, with the five-storey tower block that hosts the Science labs looming over the playground like the Royal Earlswood over the neighbouring village. "Perhaps I could have given this life more of a chance, as my parents were always telling me to," Singer wonders, over the noise. "I'd made my mind up to leave before my first day here, and so I grew up in exile in the only place I'd ever called home."

The camera shakes: perhaps Singer did not use a tripod as they wanted to be able to get away quickly if seen shooting, but the jerky effect conveys two things. The first is that this is not a major work, but one made quickly and cheaply during the pandemic, when more ambitious or elaborate filmmaking is impossible. The second is the nature of Singer's personality, at least as an adolescent: jittery, anxious, trying to assert their own opinions, tastes and desires while being deeply concerned with peer acceptance and struggling to work out how much to display of their gender non-conformity. We were in the same year at this school, both taking our GCSEs in 1998 and then going to sixth-form college in Reigate, before I moved to Brighton and Singer to London. Singer talks about alienation, boredom and loneliness, leading to a deep-seated depression. I recall these feelings well, as we shared them. How could we not, in a town like this, with its run-down high street, its lack of anything to do besides under-age drinking and chasing the dragon at house parties, the constant fear of being beaten up by resentful teenagers with little to occupy them and less to hope for?

Singer stops lingering on the playground, and talks about the early 2000s, when they and other queer people took vicious abuse in a national moral panic that culminated in a mob in Newport driving a paediatrician out of her home (and an avalanche of complaints against Chris Morris's *Brass Eye* special on Channel 4, satirising the media's role in this campaign). They take a walk that we often did together, home from school, either over the rusty railway bridge or through the subway (which, Singer wryly tells us, apparently inspired a song by *The Cure* "that's six lines long", which is commemorated with an unofficial blue plaque). Wondering what became of the school bullies and if they even *want* to know, Singer mentions a fight that they were supposed to have here, "twenty-four years ago" with "a boy from Year 10" that "I was later told got set up because I was bent". Wisely, Singer didn't show up, hiding at my house instead, not long after I'd become their only friend, and not long before I became rather more than that. Filming the trains from the bridge, Singer reflects on how often they left during their teens (partly because it was so much easier to bunk the fares back then) and on their permanent departure in 2000, which seemed to freeze the town's development in Singer's mind, almost as if it didn't exist when they weren't there.

Horley *has* changed, of course, but glacially compared to the nearest cities. Singer notes the Gatwick Islamic Centre, pointedly named after the nowhere-place of the nearby airport rather than the long-established town populated overwhelmingly by white, middle-class people who always return Conservative MPs and councillors, shown on a board in the centre. (If Singer had kept up with local news, they might have heard about people vandalising the Centre back in 2012, throwing alcohol and eggs at it and scrawling graffiti on it as worshippers observed Ramadan.) They stop at a bookmaker, which used to be a record shop in the 1990s, where the staff introduced us to the kind of artists whose works now make up the soundtracks for Singer's films: *Fennesz, Mogwai, Underground Resistance*, etc. Singer tells us briefly about "the only thing in the town I ever loved", and how it closed down "when Tesco and then Amazon started selling CDs and the shop couldn't keep flogging singles to kids on their way home from school to subsidise them selling weird electronic records to people like me". There's an air of smug superiority to this, coming from Singer's relief at successfully leaving a place "without culture" and becoming something like the person they wanted to be. They show us the old library, closed down and unoccupied, but not the larger one recently opened at the other end of the high street, but one doesn't have to know this to suspect the filmmaker is more concerned with weaving a story about their self than their surroundings.

After pausing at the memorial and thinking about the role that local and national mythology around the two world wars, and rhetoric around patriotism and terrorism more generally, played in binding the Conservative (or anti-Labour) voter bloc in December's election, Singer enters the recreation ground (or "Rec" as we called it). This hosts the annual funfair and fireworks, with a skate park and a tennis courts, and used to have a little gazebo that, as Singer recalls, had "No Gays" daubed across it almost as soon as it opened. Singer focuses on the empty space where it stood, using double exposure (a bit of a cliché in this type of film) to take us back to the past, with two people kissing inside a similar wooden structure (presumably filmed elsewhere, although Singer doesn't say so), looking nervously to camera in fear of being seen and, almost certainly, verbally or physically attacked.

The dialogue stops and the music intensifies in *A Return*'s most powerful sequence, as Singer fades to the same people in a dark indoor space. Both would be read as male: one helps the other to dress as a woman in a wig and make-up, soft pink dress and stockings, and then they kiss again. It reminded me of Carolee Schneemann's *Fuses* and other 1960s experimental films, as Singer shows the full pleasure of this sexual act and then cuts to close-ups of a hand moving across stockings or caressing a false breast, lips touching and bodies pressing. Readers might have guessed by now that the cross-dresser was Singer and the male figure was me, in the most loving moments of a furtive relationship that began in our final year at school and ended in our first year at sixth-form college.

The film captures the incredible joy of the secretive sex, which took place at my little home on the Langshott estate when my mother was out (and often used her clothes), but not Singer's constant vacillation on whether they wanted a relationship, nor their refusal to allow any public expression of it even after they came out, at college. It makes no mention of how Singer began dating a woman in summer 1999: my problem was not, as some of my friends suggested, that Singer had been "pretending to be gay" because "it's cool" (trust me, I still have a scar on my head that says it wasn't, not in our town) but that it began when we were together, with no agreement about whether our relationship was open, and if it was, *how* open. For all the time we'd spent together, I was swiftly dropped; Singer's relationship with the woman didn't last long, as they met a man as soon as they started at Goldsmiths. I don't know if Singer is with anyone now, but there are no more mentions of romance or relationships in *A Return*: perhaps their artistic career crowded out everyone and everything else.

Singer finishes the film walking along the River Mole − as we often did, holding hands when we felt certain no-one could see. As they wander through an alley past an old pub to the yard of the 14th century church, they reflect on reconciliation, wondering how much of their identity is built on their rejection of the town, and its rejection of them. The light is fading, and the multi-coloured burn gradually consumes the 16mm stock, before whiting out and bringing the film to a close, scored by a beautiful ambient piece by German composer Wolfgang Voigt − specifically, 'Königsforst 6', to which I introduced the filmmaker on its release back in 1999. Hearing one of my favourite pieces of music in this context, I thought about the catharsis for which *A Return* is aiming. Its conclusion felt hollow to me, as Singer never expressed anything but contempt for the town when living in it, and I doubt the sincerity of the apparent peace made with it at the end: this makes the film feel like the cinematic equivalent of sticking a Union Jack on top of an asylum and rebranding it as luxury flats.

Perhaps I'm not the best judge. Like Singer, I've moved on, first to Brighton and then Berlin, and have had several long-term relationships since then. But I still remember how they never really apologised for the way they treated me as a teenager. And then it occurred to me: could this be intended as some form of belated apology? Because who is this film *for*, if not for me? Or, more likely, for Singer to assuage some longstanding guilt? And is all art, at its core, primarily for the person who makes it?

FREEDOM DAY

Monday

Ryan Still up for cans in the park this arvo?   09.30

Red Star News have just asked me
to document this protest at Parliament Square.
Wanna come and film it? Paid gig! 😀   09.32

Florence Oh man, it's my day off   09.33

Ryan What's the protest?   09.34

Anti-lockdown   09.34

Ryan God, those guys are unhinged   09.34

Florence What are they protesting for? They've got
everything they wanted   09.35

That's what Red Star want me to ask. You in?   09.35

Ryan It's like 400 degrees   09.36

I know, I've got sun cream.
Beers on me after, I promise   09.37

Florence Alright, as it's you   09.39

Florence I guess I'm providing moral support or something   09.39

Florence Can't stay all day though, door-knocking for the Renters Union at 5   09.40

God, even thinking about knocking
on doors gives me PTSD   09.40

Ryan, you in?   09.41

Ryan Yeah, I love spending my days with a bunch of cranks 😊   09.43

We know babe xx   09.43

Parliament Square at 11 to set up x   09.43

Flo and I are here, where are you?   11.02

Ryan Five minutes x   11.04

★

I was already pissed off with Ryan for showing up late, although to be fair, I did kind of spring this on him, and maybe we'd have been better off swigging a few cans in London Fields than talking to the 'White Carnation' lot. We watched the police keeping everyone in the square as we set up over the road – Flo said it might annoy people if they thought we were filming in secret. Their stickers were everywhere, up and down the escalators at Westminster Tube, all over the lampposts and the shops, on the screen of the cashpoint outside Tesco Express so no-one could use it, complaining about muzzles and pubs being closed while borders were open, saying 'There is no pandemic' and 'The media is the virus'. Ryan went to tear one of them off the cashpoint; Flo told him it wasn't worth it, and we went to the protest, camera in hand.

'We're here today at Parliament Square on what Boris Johnson and the Tory press have long been calling 'Freedom Day'. For many of us, this "freedom" is terrifying – it means exposure to the virus and, if you're especially vulnerable, going back into 'shielding' without any of the support, however inadequate, provided by the government last year. But for the people here, the lifting of virtually all Covid-19 restrictions is not enough – they're protesting against the possibility of future lockdowns, the fact that organisations such as Transport for London are still making it mandatory to wear face masks, and the ongoing vaccination programme. It's thirty degrees and tempers are already flaring – we're going to talk to a few people about *why* they're demonstrating, today of all days.'

A few people were looking at us as I tried to get the measure of the crowd, and who might be good to talk to. They looked quite old, lots of them, bald red men with England tattoos, retired white couples, a bunch of old punks in tight black dresses, one holding a massive black flag with an 'A' scrawled in red in the middle. Ryan noticed someone in a *Dead Kennedys* T-shirt, shook his head and said, 'He obviously hasn't fucking *listened* to them.' There were younger people too, a few looked like students, and hippie women in tie-dye dresses. I thought I saw a couple of journalists, one who pops up on *Newsnight* sometimes to complain about 'wokeness'. Then I noticed Flo glancing around anxiously to see where the cops were, and what they were up to – they didn't look like they were gearing up to bash anyone's heads in, like they did at the Sarah Everard vigil, but I wouldn't have bet against it, not with the new law on their side. Anyway, most of the protestors were curious rather than aggressive towards us, though I heard a couple of shouts – 'Crooked media!' and 'Biased broadcasting corporation!'

"Do we look like we're from the fucking BBC?" muttered Ryan. A man and a woman, who I guessed were in their sixties and married, came up to me: "Who are you filming for?"

"Red Star News, we're a small YouTube channel covering British politics. Is it okay if I ask why you're here today?"

"Yes," said the man. "It's because I'm worried about all the socialist policies this government is putting through under the cover of this 'pandemic'."

"Which socialist policies?" asked Ryan.

"Don't you know?" the man replied. "I thought you lot were covering politics." Before Ryan or I could answer, he went on. "Putting us under all this surveillance, making us all take tests and wear masks all the time, making us have a passport before we can go anywhere."

Should I ask the obvious question? I took a breath. "What do you think socialism is?"

"It's taking away our freedom. It's stopping us moving about and controlling every aspect of people's lives, like the Russians did. It's throwing free money at people who scrounge off the state while people who want to work aren't allowed to get ahead."

My mind couldn't help drifting back to that dark, cold winter, a year and a half ago. *Hello, I'm Sarah, I'm with the local Labour Party,* doors slammed in our faces, Barnet, Crawley, Milton Keynes, *I'm not voting for Corbyn, he supports the IRA,* old men in Yorkshire screaming down the phone about *Al-Qaeda, the bloody Muslims* and *that fucking second referendum...* all the wild shit people believed, yet you weren't allowed to ask: *Who's been telling you this?*

"You don't think the government should support people during lockdowns?" I asked.

"There shouldn't *be* any lockdowns!"

"There's not any more," I replied. A crowd was gathering.

"No, because they realised we aren't going to let them get away with it."

"And we're not going to let them get away with 'Covid passports' either," came another voice. "I was dead against ID cards back in the day, and I'm not standing for this."

"I was against ID cards as well," said Ryan, "and I agree about Covid passports. The government shouldn't be pushing it and Starmer shouldn't support it."

Then a shout: "That Starmer's just another commie!"

"He loves the EUSSR!"

I tried not to laugh at Ryan's disbelief: "You think Starmer's a communist?"

"Of course he's a communist, he takes the bloody knee!"

"That doesn't make him a communist," said Flo. 'Ten minutes later, he was on TV saying we shouldn't defund the police.'

"Too bloody right we shouldn't defund the police," said our interviewee's wife. "They've had enough taken from them already. We all have."

"Starmer's just the same as Johnson," said the man. "They both want to chuck more money at the cops for their police state. He didn't even vote against that bill to ban protests."

"Jeremy Corbyn spoke at the Kill the Bill rallies," said Ryan.

"And he spoke out against vaccine passports," added Flo.

"Never mind about Jeremy bloody Corbyn," came a voice from behind me, laughing. "You've got your new man now – nice and electable."

"Trust me, I'm no more likely to vote for that prick Starmer than you are," said Ryan, smiling. I thought about how depressing the London elections had been – going from voting for a Green New Deal, free broadband, keeping freedom of movement and abolishing more tuition fees in December 2019 to that YouTuber who said he'd tell Boris Johnson to 'shush' in May 2021, giving my Assembly vote to the Communist Party no-hopers and abstaining on the constituency because, really, if the Greens were the best option then *what was the point?*

"You supported Corbyn, did you?"

"I did, yeah," replied Ryan.

"I did too, in 2017," said our interviewee. "I switched to the Tories because Boris said he'd get Brexit done. All that noise about taking back control – but it was control for *them*, not for us."

"You thought the guy from the Bullingdon Club was a man of the people?"

"I thought Boris cared about freedom," said the man. "If your guy Corbyn was truly a man of the people, like he kept saying, he'd be here with us. Like his brother. I wish he was mayor – he'd be better than that Sad-Sack Khan and all his crap about face masks."

"Oh no," Flo whispered as I wondered whether I'd ever seen Corbyn describe himself thus, and remembered when Khan had said Labour deserved to lose in 2019. "Is Piers coming?" she asked, referring to Jeremy's loose cannon of a brother.

"Look," said Ryan to the man we were interviewing. "If 'they' – the establishment, the deep state, whatever – wanted a socialist government, don't you think they would've just let Labour win the last election?"

"Too obvious," said the man. "And anyway, Johnson is their puppet."

"This is the most right-wing government we've ever had!" Flo replied, incredulous. "They've banned protest, they're censoring the press, they're making war crimes legal, they're stopping migration except for the rich." Ryan gestured at Flo not to take it further, as I read some home-made signs: 'It's not a pandemic, it's an IQ test' / 'Leave our DNA alone' / 'Unity is freedom'. As they began chanting 'No more lockdowns', Ryan whispered into my ear: "You know Ian Brown from the Stone Roses refers to Starmer as 'Sir Tier Stasi'?" I laughed. "He also calls Chris Whitty 'Piss Shitty', but we all do that. Right?"

"Don't make me laugh, you'll get me in trouble." I realised I needed to get all this on film. "Whose puppet?" I asked.

"The state. The media. Big business."

"Well, I agree with you there," said Ryan.

"Me too," added Flo. "But why would business want everyone locked down?"

"So we buy their shit online!"

"And they don't have to pay their staff!"

"And we get taxed for their furlough!"

"What tax increases have there been?" I asked.

"None *yet...*"

"Did you read about that on Facebook?" asked Ryan.

"No, it was in the paper."

"You can't just let this virus run riot," I said. "The case numbers are through the roof!"

"Have any of *you* had it?"

"I did," said Flo.

"And what happened?"

"I self-isolated for ten days."

"Were you sick?"

"Quite sick, yes."

"Did you have the vaccine?"

"Yes, I work in healthcare," replied Flo.

"But you still got ill?" a man asked. "And you still don't see how they're lying to you?"

"Trust me, it would've been a lot worse without it."

"Trust *you*?" said a man in the crowd. "You're a bloody doctor!"

"I'm not a doctor, I work in commissioning. I'm just based in a hospital," Flo told him, trying to keep her voice down. "I see where you're coming from, but nobody who's *seen* what's been happening in the NHS would say this isn't real."

"Are you familiar with the Nuremburg Code?"

"One of my old lecturers died," said Ryan. "He wouldn't have if they'd locked down earlier. We could all see what was happening in Spain and Italy."

"It's a global conspiracy!"

More people were gathering, and I was starting to worry – it wasn't just the blissed-out hippies and the old *Daily Mail* couples, but skinheads draped in England flags and Union Jacks, who were getting angrier. Protestors began to swarm around us, and then the cops: I had flashbacks to them pinning me down and putting me in an armlock at the Everard vigil, horses everywhere at the Kill the Bill protests just after that, and at the BLM demo on Trafalgar Street last summer, that antifa demo in Whitechapel in 2013, the police arresting us all and making us march past the EDL. I couldn't tell who the police were planning to protect here, apart from themselves, but they started forming a circle around us.

"Are you going to kettle us again?" asked Ryan. "There's some women for you to beat up!"

"You going to arrest him for that, officer?" came a voice. "Or are you on their side?"

"You think the police are on *our* side?" I asked.

"Shit, they're chucking bottles!" said Flo.

On the other side of the Square, we saw a big group of men squaring up to the cops. Chants of 'Shame on police' and 'Arrest Boris Johnson', with people yelling about his 'crimes against humanity'. Ryan whispered: 'At least we agree on something.' Everyone around us – police and protestors – rushed over to the battle. Flo grabbed Ryan's shoulder to stop him from joining them. "Sorry," he said. "Just habit."

A policeman stopped us. "I think you should leave."

"We've got every right to film here," I replied.

"That's not much good if they take your camera and beat you up. Seriously, you're lucky they didn't. We see this lot every weekend and they're only getting worse."

I put the camera away, as Ryan started filming the fracas on his iPhone. A bottle flew past a little boy on a man's shoulders and smashed in front of a police line. "What are they guarding the Churchill statue for?" asked Flo as the skinheads with St. George's Cross tattoos lined up in front of it. There were people screaming about vaccines, yelling about 'death shots', and it looked like they were starting to fight each other; when the chants of 'hang the traitors' began, I knew we had to get out. Ryan started tweeting about the violence, adding 'More on Red Star News at 7pm'. I yelled at him to put his fucking phone away and come with us. He did, and as we backed out of the Square, he said: "I know I *always* say this, but imagine what this would've been like if Corbyn had won." I couldn't help thinking, *maybe it's best that we lost.* But I hated myself for it, and kept it to myself.

And then, as we headed back to the Tube station, we saw someone else interviewing people on the fringes of the protest. Peter Jordan.

"What's *he* doing here?" asked Flo.

"It's for his horrible YouTube channel," said Ryan.

"I haven't seen it," replied Flo.

"I have," I said. "He did a long rant about cancel culture with that alt-right YouTuber – Mitch something – because nobody went to his book launch. It was on Zoom for fuck's sake, no-one wants to go to those any more."

"Mitch O'Donnell? That Trump supporter?" Flo asked. "How did he get in with him?"

"Usual way," I said. "Got in with the 'gender critical' lot after he started posting transphobic shit on Facebook, and then went off on one about how the 'woke left' want to silence debate after people called him out on it. So obviously the alt-right love-bombed him, and that's why we now have 'Rivers of Truth' with Peter S. Jordan."

"Rivers of Truth?" asked Flo. "Did he name it after the Enoch Powell speech?"

"He's started blogging for the *Telegraph*, so it makes sense."

Peter was giving out leaflets to people he spoke to: my mind flashed back to 2013, seeing him selling the *Socialist Worker* outside Whitechapel station before he got his head kicked in, first by the EDL and then by the cops. I didn't want to know what he was handing out now – the SWP newspapers had been bad enough, especially after the Comrade Delta scandal – and I was trying to steer us away when he caught my eye, and then Ryan squared up to him.

"Are you two still seeing each other?" he asked Ryan and me.

"We broke up years ago, but we're still mates," said Ryan, holding my hand. "And comrades."

"*Comrades*," replied Peter. "Still cosplaying the Russian revolution?" Flo muttered a *fuck you* under her breath. He didn't notice, luckily, as he said: "Come and join the White Carnation, if you want a movement that's not just full of sneering liberals doing prole-face." I said nothing.

"Want to talk about why *you* joined it on camera?" said Ryan. "We're filming the protest too."

I was furious. We'd never talked about this, but surely, he knew our audience would go nuts if we got Peter on, even if it was just because we'd chanced on him like this. Ryan took out his phone, and I suspected he was about to run a poll about this on Twitter when Peter interrupted.

"Wouldn't you rather come and debate me on *my* show?" asked Peter. "Let's test your 'science' with facts and logic. And we can talk about how you lot ended up supporting the Tories as they put everyone under house arrest."

"We're always critical of government policy!" I replied. "We've done shows on the lockdowns, how they opened up for the wrong reasons, how they haven't given enough support to shielders, renters, the homeless, freelancers and key workers. What kind of freedom do they get?"

"Why don't you come on and discuss it?"

"Because you'll set all your fascist fans on us on Twitter?" said Ryan.

"Still calling anyone you disagree with a fascist?"

"No – just fascists," replied Ryan.

"Whatever," said Peter. "Never mind, I've got real people to talk to."

Peter turned his back and went to talk to some old punks. I looked back as the police struggled to calm down the protestors on the other side of the Square. The bottles seemed to have stopped flying at least, they'd cordoned off the most aggressive people from the ones who hadn't come for a fight. We walked back to the Tube, heads down, making sure not to put on our masks until we were well out of sight. I was surprised Ryan didn't want to talk about what looked like a new type of fascism, let alone that he didn't bring up my promise to buy us all beers, but I guess we all just wanted to go home.

A MANIFESTO
(FOR THE) UNSEEN

You sat in those gardens most weekday afternoons, in the early autumn and late spring. In the summer, you went back to your parents, despite hating your hometown: you always said you couldn't stand hot weather, the pressure to have *fun*. You just wanted to be on your own. Your pen and paper weren't quite an anachronism – some of the students had their own laptops, but they were too heavy to carry around, and you said you'd never stop writing your manifestos by hand. You wouldn't reveal their content, at least not exactly, and maybe no-one ever saw them, but you were convinced they were going to change the world. At the dawn of the 21st century, though, you were reading your way into the 20th, the Russian Futurists rather than the Italians because, you said, you wanted revolution rather than reaction. The end of the Soviet dream, just a decade before we met, didn't seem to register with any of your fellow students, which you said was strange given that it was the defining event of their young lives, and sad given how much it had narrowed their horizons, even if they didn't realise it like you did.

More than anything, you wanted to find a way to break out of boredom, and forming a band hadn't worked. Your occasional discourses about pop (if not *popular)* music, be it yours or a handful of other people's, were the only times you mentioned any new form of creativity since the Second World War, though, and it seemed like you were just setting yourself up to fail like the modern authors you revered, and not to fail better. At least the names of those inter-war writers killed by militias or dictatorships would survive the talentless apparatchiks who snuffed them out, you said, and their works still made a difference to people. But when a course mate told you, in those dreamy, doomy weeks as our finals started and the war broke out, despite your protests against it, that you were "not intelligent enough" to succeed where the people you read had failed, and died slowly, been killed by the state, or resorted to the fatal dead-end of red terrorism, you just shrugged, as if to say, pessimistically, *we'll see.*

After graduation, you moved to a different city at the other end of the country and cut ties with everyone. It was still the case back then, just about, that losing contact was the passive option. It was impossible to imagine you on Facebook or Myspace, a few years later, casually keeping in touch with anyone who visited your 'profile'. It's understandable and unsurprising: however you saw yourself, other people viewed you as lost, sad, or strange. Nobody ever heard of you dating or could imagine you in a relationship. Nobody even heard you express an interest in anyone – only your complaints about your Saturday job in a bookshop. You must have kept writing: poetry, diaries, short stories. Perhaps you even published them, in tiny journals. Maybe you chose a pseudonym, referencing one of your inspirations, using your sharp sense of humour that few people saw and even fewer understood. But how on Earth did you make a living – and how did you *live* – beyond the rarefied confines of the campus?

People looked for your writing – your manifestos – your *name* for years, in vain. They searched for you online, convinced that you "must have done *something*", even if it was going mad, or killing someone, most likely yourself. Surely that would show up on Google, even if it was just a brief report in a local paper. But no: nothing for your name and 'manifesto', or anything else. You wouldn't have settled into a "normal" life, you always said there was no point. But where were you? Had you changed your identity? Found a way to do your *something* in secret? Or simply vanished? You were always fascinated by people who disappeared.

At least a decade ago, a dream of you. In a national garden alone, at night, a light aircraft flew overhead, towards a monument. The monument had its back to me but I knew it was of you. The plane crashed; the statue went up in flames. There were no ashes, nothing. Its meaning was obvious: not just the *burning ambition* but you, blazing into the ether, after you went from being someone who everyone talked about all the time to someone no-one had even thought about for years.

At a tiny London gallery, years later, *A Manifesto (for the) Unseen*. Its tone felt familiar, full of contradictions: declamatory yet self-effacing, witty yet deadly serious, proudly anonymous yet clearly written by an irrepressible ego. *Was it you?* One of those 'collectives' that is actually just one person, at least to start, hopefully becoming a 'movement' if you find that rare thing: people who don't just share your view of the world but also your conception of how to change it. It talked about the power of refusing an online 'presence' and of working in secret, hinting at the surveillance culture that came with the 'War on Terror', telling people not to do the deep state's work for it via social media, and how dismantling Web 2.0 would make a better world. It should not just be old white male men like

Pynchon or Salinger who were allowed to reject 'visibility', declared the manifesto, but anyone, *everyone* oppressed by it. This was the first step towards creating a culture that would generate a *Communist Manifesto,* a *What is to be Done* or a *Revolution of Everyday Life* for our time, raising the same questions as Marx and Engels, Lenin or the Situationists, producing answers for the 21st century and reversing the disastrous inequality that came with the failure of socialism, unencumbered by an intellectual terrain dominated by the 'Great Men' who haunted your History degree.

In another contradiction, it was distributed online – with no names and no contacts. Asked who wrote it, the gallery attendant just shrugged, and nobody there responded to emails about its author – most likely on your instructions, if indeed it was you, setting yourself up to fail through being untraceable. Looking for you on Facebook was pointless, although one could almost imagine you on Twitter, one of those anonymous far-left weirdos with a cartoon avatar and a pun on some obscure Marxist theorist for a handle, or maybe even on Instagram, posting nothing with a human face. If you are on there, hopefully you'll be left alone: if you are still living, and still *writing*, it doubtless depends on that solitude.

Who knows if you will ever read this, but it's so unsettling to think that now, you will still only be forty years old. As an undergraduate, you were determined to die long before then, actually die, but only after you had done *something,* as the tiny circle of people who invested in you in your small suburban hometown hoped you would – not just the symbolic death of obscurity. You always carried a paperback, often Kafka or Nietzsche, and struck at the tantalising nature of those authors who died, or were killed, young. What *didn't* they get to write? What *weren't* they able to publish? What did they decide not to keep – if they even got to make that decision? What were the ethics of their friends defying their dying wishes for destruction?

If you're still around most likely you wish you weren't, wish you were living in an age in which you might write yourself into a heroic death. But replicating those legends in another time, and not being purged but merely ignored, seems like the feeblest form of failure, and far too simple for someone who always had to make things difficult. Power just ignores writers now, you said, having realised that allowing criticism to be aired but to ignore it, setting up structures to ensure its marginalisation, was easier and far more effective than killing heretics, allowing the veneer of democracy to be maintained. You said Camus saved your life, long before you got to your hall of residence, but you didn't think the existentialists' conclusion that life was pointless was an endpoint. Rather, it was liberating: if everything means nothing, then you can do anything. Perhaps it wasn't fair to demand you do *something,* maybe that pressure didn't help you to write meaning into your life, or life in general, or to work out how writing might change the world in the new millennium. On those terms, it's no wonder that you should *want* to fail, better or not: the question of whether you 'did something' is no less absurd than any other, and I can't imagine anything you'd hate more than a monument to you.

A TYPICAL DAY

FADE IN:

SCENE 1. INT. THE MOT CENTRE - LATE MORNING

JULIA, 32, is on reception, eating from a plastic box as she works. next to her computer are a phone and piles of paper. PRANAV, 55, enters, wearing dirty overalls.

            PRANAV
Morning Jules - how was your appointment?

            JULIA
Fine, thanks.

            PRANAV
Clean bill of health?

            JULIA
Yeah, nothing to worry about.

PRANAV

How's it going here?

JULIA

Oh, you know. Same old, same old.

PRANAV

Yeah, I know the feeling. How was your evening class?

JULIA

Not bad. We worked on story structure.

PRANAV

Oh yes? Tell me how you structure a story.

JULIA

They said you should start your characters in their normal world, wanting to change something; the story is how they go about it. They take a few risks, there's a crunch point and then a conclusion, where you find out if they've got what they want, and what that means.

PRANAV

Dreaming of the big time?

JULIA

Not really, I just write for myself.

PRANAV gets his jacket.

Where are you off to?

> **JULIA**
> Just popping next door for a sandwich, I won't be long.

The phone rings: JULIA answers. PRANAV nods as he exits, to ask if she wants anything – she waves to say no.

> **JULIA**
> Hello, The MOT Centre, Julia speaking. (Pause) Julia. (Pause) No, not Julian. Julia. How can I help? (She looks through the papers) It won't be ready until Friday, I think my colleague told you. (Pause) He's just popped out for lunch. (Pause) There isn't anyone else to speak to. We'll call you when it's done.

The caller hangs up. JULIA angrily puts down the phone and sighs. She stares at it, with tears in her eyes, for a moment. Then she sees PRANAV return with a sandwich and tries to compose herself.

> **PRANAV**
> You alright?

> **JULIA**
> Yeah, just the usual. "Don't you mean Julian?" No, I fucking well don't.

PRANAV

People struggle with my name too.

JULIA

Yeah, I know. Honestly, when I get this kind
of aggro, I just want to walk out.

PRANAV

I know the feeling. But you can't quit,
it just lets them win. And besides, you've
barely been here six weeks. Who was it?

JULIA

Trevor Jordan, again. About his Mondeo.

PRANAV

Oh God, that guy. Tell him it'll be ready by
Friday.

JULIA

If he calls again, do you mind dealing with
him?

PRANAV

Yeah, sure.

PRANAV goes back to the garage; JULIA goes back
to her lunch, and her computer. She is disturbed
by a knock at the door. She looks up: it's a
middle-aged man with flowers. She nods at him
to come in.

MAN

Afternoon - hope I'm not disturbing you. I just wanted to thank you both for the bang-up job you did with my car last week.

JULIA

I didn't do anything, it was my colleague.

MAN

You were a very courteous receptionist.

JULIA

Well, I'm glad you think so (Laughs)... That's very kind of you, anyway.

The MAN gives the flowers to JULIA, and stands at the desk, holding her gaze for a little too long.

MAN

I'd be best off. Thanks again.

JULIA

No, thank you.

The MAN leaves. JULIA sighs, puts the flowers down on the desk and looks at them. Then she goes to the kitchen and fills a vase with water. PRANAV enters.

PRANAV

Who gave you those?

JULIA

Mr. Wilson. The guy with the Clio.

PRANAV

Looks like you've got an admirer...

JULIA

He said he was pleased with the service. Maybe he's just bored with the wife.

JULIA takes the flowers back to her desk, putting them next to the monitor. PRANAV sits in a chair, eating his lunch. JULIA's mobile phone bleeps to say she has an email. She reads it.

JULIA

Oh my God!

PRANAV

What is it?

JULIA

It's Nick from my night school. He says he was talking to an agent about our class, and the agent wants to read my stories!

PRANAV

I thought you just wrote for yourself?

JULIA

Well yes, mostly, but if someone wants to

look at them... But I don't know... I'm not
sure they're ready.

PRANAV

Oh, come on — what's the worst that could
happen? (JULIA thinks.) Maybe you'll end up
writing a bestseller. Like J.K. Rowling or
something.

JULIA

Well, I'd rather not be like J.K. Rowling.

PRANAV

Why not?

JULIA

It's a long story. But I should do it, you're
right.

PRANAV

Not on our time, though.

JULIA

What? Of course not.

PRANAV

I've seen you, when you think I'm not paying
attention. Surfing the web when it's quiet is
one thing — bringing your own work is quite
another.

JULIA

I only do it when I've finished everything else. And even then, hardly ever.

PRANAV

I'm not trying to stop you - I want you to do well and I can replace you if I have to. I just don't think you should be doing it when I'm paying you.

JULIA

Yeah, I know. Sorry, Pranav.

PRANAV

Your heart's not really in this, is it?

JULIA

I turn up on time, looking presentable, I do everything you ask without complaining and I'm polite to the customers - isn't that enough?

A loud bang is heard from the garage.

Shit, what was that?

PRANAV sticks his head around the door.

PRANAV

Just something falling over, it's nothing.

JULIA

It's always nothing.

PRANAV

What do you mean?

JULIA

We turn up every morning, just to pay the
bills, knowing every day will be the same.

PRANAV

I'm fine with that. If it's not, it usually
means a massive pain in the arse.

JULIA

Today it's fairly quiet.

PRANAV

Quiet enough for us to chat like this.

JULIA

But even on a day like today, things happen
that make it different to the next, and
they're not all bad. Like that guy bringing
us flowers.

PRANAV

Bringing you flowers.

JULIA

You're not jealous, are you?

PRANAV

No, it's fine.

JULIA

Don't worry — I wasn't interested in him.

PRANAV

I'm a married man, Julia!

JULIA

So was he, probably. (They laugh.) But let's say I used him in one of my Creative Writing exercises. The Opening is me being bored, waiting for something to do.

PRANAV

The usual.

JULIA

Then the man gives me flowers, and I start flirting with him.

PRANAV

Again...

JULIA

How very dare you? (Laughs) Maybe he leaves a business card or something.

PRANAV

Would you go on a date with him?

JULIA

If I liked him, sure. Then anything could happen. But it didn't, and it doesn't – guys like that never leave their wives, and certainly not for someone like me. Most of the time, there isn't a story.

PRANAV

I guess the man coming in, giving you the flowers, you politely thanking him and getting back to work is a story of sorts.

JULIA

Yes, but it's not very dramatic.

PRANAV

Yeah, why would anybody want to watch that?

JULIA

And that's the problem, isn't it? For most of us, most of the time, every day is just an Opening, and maybe an Inciting Incident that doesn't go anywhere. A few weeks ago – you weren't here – a customer was so rude to me, giving me all kinds of transphobic bullshit, that I walked out.

PRANAV

Why didn't you tell me?

JULIA

Because I went outside, thought "What now?"

and walked back in again. I guess I could have taken the risk, but you can't get on the dole if you quit your job.

PRANAV

So, we're all stuck with our boring lives.

JULIA

Unless something unexpected happens.

They pause.

Nothing happens...

They wait...

Nothing happens...

JULIA

Let's go back to my writing exercise. If I write about something weird happening – I dunno, one of the cars turns out to be a spaceship or capable of time travel, or something – it just seems contrived.

PRANAV

And it's been done before.

JULIA

And it seems like I'm saying most people's lives are too dull to be worth talking about. Let's say I make a story about a typical day.

I might use that transphobic customer as my jumping-off point. But then it'd look like I was casting the public as a bunch of hateful monsters.

PRANAV

Plenty of them are.

JULIA

Well, Johnson doesn't win a landslide without them. But "the public" are a lot more complicated than that.

PRANAV

So, write something longer. A sitcom.

JULIA

About a trans woman and a British Asian man working together in a garage? I can see the headlines now...

PRANAV

'Woke Beeb spends YOUR taxes on leftie propaganda!'

JULIA

That'd be the nicest one. It'd be even worse if I did a drama for Channel Four.

PRANAV

They wouldn't show anything like that now.

JULIA

Maybe I should pitch Britain's Worst Scroungers. But then I'd hate myself.

PRANAV

Maybe it's better not to sell out. Why not stick to your short stories?

JULIA

I think I will. People don't mind so much when characters in a book just sit around talking. Film audiences aren't so keen.

PRANAV

You could try writing a play.

JULIA

Yeah, that might work. I just need to find something that'll set up the right story.

The phone rings. JULIA answers.

Sorry, I'm afraid you've got the wrong number.

JULIA puts down the phone.

Whatever it is, it's not coming to me today.

PRANAV

You'll just have to think harder, won't you? (Smiles) At home.

PRANAV checks his watch.

> Sugar, is that the time? I'd better get back
> to Mr. Jordan's car, I don't want him flipping
> his lid at us.

JULIA

Nobody wants to see that.

PRANAV goes back into the garage. JULIA finishes
her lunch in front of the computer, clearly
looking at the internet. She looks at a pile of
papers, the top of which is a screenplay marked
'A Typical Day' by Julia James, shakes her head,
sighs, put it down and starts filling out some
forms instead.

FADE OUT:

THE END

STILL LIGHT, OUTSIDE

The waves were still crashing, indifferent to her fate. For a while, she could hear them receding as she walked away, but she stopped noticing their sounds as she focused on putting one foot in front of the other: all she could manage right now. She had no idea what time it was, having left everything at home except £50 in cash – more than half of which she'd spent on the train ticket – and her front door key, in case she changed her mind. She hadn't expected to, but now she was glad of her precaution.

There was no pavement here. No cars either, not at this time. The dark was terrifying but, paradoxically, she felt like the pitch-black might provide some sanctuary. She still hoped, for quite different reasons than an hour ago, that nobody would encounter her, as the familiar anxieties about injury and assault, something that couldn't have mattered to her less when she was standing on the beach, had kicked back in. In the distance, first a speck, soon a sun, a light. An old joke drifted into the blankness of her mind, about a moth on its way to see a psychiatrist, and she half-laughed at the memory, something so silly on a night so serious. Rain swept in from the beach, alerting her again to the water, lashing at her face. Suddenly she wished a car would pass over the horizon so it could take her somewhere safe, somewhere dry, though she still didn't want to have to explain to anyone what she was doing here.

It felt like forever to reach the light. When she did it carried just one simple message: Pendleton's. It stood at the front of the lawn, a round bulb with this name printed on it, before a little white fence and gate. The lights in the building were off, and there was just one car parked outside. She had enough illumination to work out it was a Bed and Breakfast but not enough to tell if it was closed for the off-season. It was bad form, she knew, to ring at this unknown but clearly unsociable hour – but what else could she do?

No answer, obviously. But why would that light still be on, outside, if no-one was there? She rang again. Silence. She sat on the doorstep and wept, like she had on the beach, where she had stood and faced the waves. She waited, gazing past the road and over the cliff-face to the sea. Flickering thoughts of going back, then: footsteps. The sound of a switch, the light in the hallway. She sprang to her feet, wiped away the tears. She'd worn no make-up tonight, not caring if anyone recognised her, so there'd be no smudges and hopefully no trace of her distress. A figure came to the door, and from behind the glass what sounded like an old woman's voice: *Who's there?*

"Please let me in," she said. "It's dark, and I'm freezing."

Are you alone? came the voice behind the door.

"Yes, I swear on my life!" she replied, mentally adding *for what it's worth.*

The door opened.

She stared at the old woman for a moment. So much life, and who knew how much *living*, in that thin, curly white hair, with her sunken blue eye and wrinkles, the cardigan and skirt that looked years, or even decades worn. Was this a future she wanted? She wasn't sure.

"Don't just stand there – you'll catch your death!"

She tried not to laugh at the grim irony, stepped inside and saw the clock: 3.23am.

"What on Earth are you doing out here, on your own, at this time of night?"

"It's a long story."

"Do you need to use the phone?"

"I'd rather lie down for a while if that's okay with you?"

"Of course. I don't have any bookings, so you can have a bed."

"I don't have much money."

"I don't need any. Follow me."

The old lady took her upstairs and showed her an empty bedroom.

"The bathroom is along the corridor to the right. The floorboards are a bit creaky, so if you use it, try not to make too much noise. Otherwise, sleep well."

"I will. Thanks so much."

The old lady retired to her room and she was left alone. She didn't even turn on the lamp, just put her change and keys on the bedside table and climbed beneath the covers.

Although exhausted by the night, she had expected sleeplessness, her mind raking over failed ambitions and broken relationships. As it happened, she soon fell asleep, and lapsed into a recurring dream, or at least a dream with a recurring ending, the same dream she'd endured many times since her teens. It always began the same way: she would be on her own or with one other person, the location varied but she was always lost, out of her depth. It always ended the same way too, but the details in-between changed each time. Tonight, she was on a beach, alone, naked, at night, with footsteps behind and ahead of her. Seeing no-one else around, she contemplated whether those holes in the sand were from her feet or someone else's. She walked into them; they couldn't be hers as they were too small. The sand gave way and she marched towards the sea. Then the lifelong motif: a spider. It crawled out of the water, skipped over the footprints at speed, and raced up her leg, towards her AAAAAAAAHHHHHH.

She bolted upright, sweating, as she always did when she had this nightmare. She must have yelled – the few people with whom she'd ever shared a bed told her that she talked in her sleep – as there was a knock on the door.

"Are you alright?"

"Just a bad dream. Sorry to wake you."

"Do you need anything?"

"No thanks."

"Okay, well, help yourself if you do."

Footsteps going away again. Still dark outside. She tried to go back to sleep, turning, putting one leg under and the other over the duvet to cool herself, trying to regulate her breath. She met with a succession of short, savage dreams. In the first, her brother – who'd died in a car accident when she was twenty-two, and he nineteen – said he had a grave family secret to impart but vanished before doing so. In the next, a close friend, also deceased, came into her kitchen and they started making cocktails together, laughing like they used to, getting ready for a night out, opening the front door only to be met by a swirling abyss. She woke up, sad and confused, then dozed back off. In the last dream she was arrested by the secret police of some authoritarian state, which she understood to be home, and put on trial. She successfully argued her innocence of whatever charge she faced, but then had an out-of-body experience where she saw her own body, swaying gently in a barren cell. Awake, alert, she turned on the lamp and looked at the clock: 4.48am.

She turned it off and rested a little more, mercifully dreamless, until 6am or so, when she heard the old lady getting up. She opened her door just a crack, guessing correctly that this would invite her host to offer a drink. She asked for a coffee with milk, got dressed and sat on the bed, thanking the old lady for her kindness.

"Come and sit with me downstairs," said the old lady, leading her to the living room.

She hadn't noticed the décor in the bedroom, but here in the living room she did. White wallpaper that had not been changed in years, but merely painted over; an equally antiquated carpet, in need of a deep clean, and thick-set brown curtains. The upholstery had floral patterns and wooden armrests, with a couple of small cushions.

"Do you want the sofa?" she asked.

"Oh no," replied the old lady, taking the armchair. "I haven't been able to sit on that since my husband died."

She curled up on the sofa with her coffee, sipping it gently. There was a long silence. The old lady looked like she might be drifting off to sleep.

"How long have you lived here?"

"Oh, more than fifty years now. Jack and I bought it just after we got married, and I've been here ever since."

"Do you have anyone looking after you?"

"My children visit from time to time, but really, I don't need much looking after." The old lady widened her eyes. "It seems like you might, though."

She held back tears. If the old lady noticed, she didn't comment.

"What brought you down here?"

"Oh... I was seeing a friend."

"It's not a very good friend who leaves you lost in the dark, is it?"

Maybe she thinks I'm a sex worker, she wondered, but her outfit of a baggy sweatshirt, jeans and trainers with no make-up surely didn't give that impression. She wondered what the old lady saw in her, why she let her into her home, why she had allowed her to stay.

"Do I need to call the police?"

"No!" she replied. "I mean... it's not like that."

"What is it like?"

"Look, if you must know... I came down here to kill myself."

"Oh... oh dear. I'm sorry to hear that."

"I've been planning it for years. As long as I can remember, really. I always thought − if life gets too much, I'll get the train to the coast, walk along until I found somewhere I wouldn't be seen, and then..." She held back more tears. "The idea was that I'd give myself time to change my mind. I thought I wouldn't, but then I got to the water and I just..."

"What stopped you?"

"I don't know. The thought of the person who found my body. If anyone did."

"Not your friends or family?"

"Them too, I guess. At the funeral." She paused. "I didn't leave any instructions."

"But you must have had something more than that? Are you married?"

"Divorced." She paused. "No children. I wanted them. He didn't."

"Are you working?"

"I'm signed off. I don't like my job anyway."

"What do you do?"

"I'm a Project Manager at an NHS Healthcare Trust."

"What does that mean?"

"Organising meetings about budget cuts, mostly."

"How long have you been doing it?" asked the old lady.

"Too long," she replied. "Over a decade."

Silence.

"What keeps you running this place?" she asked.

"I don't know what else to do," replied the old lady.

"Come on, there must be more to it than that," she said. "What got you started?"

"Well…" She half-smiled, encouraging the old lady to think back as far as possible, offering space for the anecdote to take as long as was needed. "Jack always loved meeting new people, and I wanted to live by the sea… We talked about it for years. My family moved out of London at the start of the war, and when they got back and saw how much it had been bombed, they just wanted to leave. They didn't, but they made me want to. Jack and I got married in the late Sixties and bought this place. As you can see, I haven't had it done up in a little while."

"Do you enjoy it?"

"There's hardly any business these days. But it doesn't matter."

Another, longer silence.

"I've been alone fifteen years now," said the old lady.

"I'm sorry."

"I manage well enough."

"How?"

"Most of our guests are friends, or regulars. They don't ask much, and they keep me company." The old lady sighed. "Sometimes they drive me into town, help with the shopping, take me to the cinema, that kind of thing. And my grandchildren visit every now and again."

"That sounds nice."

"It keeps me going."

She wondered, momentarily, if she might have such a steady home or such a kind group of friends when she reached her host's age. Her rent was due; she had no savings and practically no pension. She couldn't, she worried, expect even this kind of basic security, and she hated the fact that she had to hope for the death of a parent to dig her out of old-age poverty – and knew that even that would likely not fix things.

The old lady, it seemed, was dozing off. She thought back to previous times when she'd been close to coming to the coast like this, cancelled her plans saying she had a headache, lying on her bed and somehow talking herself out of it during the long, lonely insomniac nights. Feeling comfortable in the old lady's presence, she laid on the sofa and shut her eyes, for how long she didn't know. She was roused by the question: "Another cup of tea?"

"Yes, please," she replied, waking and stretching. She saw the old lady struggling to get out of the armchair and offered to make it herself. The sight of the kitchen brought back that night's dream about her long-gone friend, and she took a second to realign herself with reality, her head back in the room well before the kettle boiled. Two with milk, no sugar, pleasantly surprised that she carried them back into the lounge without shaking and spilling them. The medication, something she'd always seen as a last resort but felt she'd had to try, had limited effect on her depression – obviously, she thought, or she wouldn't be in this place – but had made her anxiety far more manageable, and she felt a serenity here that she hadn't known since, well, perhaps since she became aware of a world beyond her family home.

"Do you want to call anyone?" asked the old lady, sipping her tea.

"There's no-one to call," she replied.

"That's not true, is it? You're still young."

"I'm forty."

"That's still young." The old lady laughed a little, for the first time. "What about your parents?"

"There's only my mum, and I don't want to worry her."

"No brothers or sisters?"

"Not any more."

Silence.

"What are you going to do, then?" asked the old lady.

"What do you mean?"

"Well... How are you going to get home?"

She paused for a second. The sight, and sound, of the waves drifted back into her mind. Then she noticed the old lady looking intently at her, smiling.

"Open the curtains," the old lady suggested. She got up. "It's beautiful out."

"Yes, it looks it." The old lady smiled. "Do you need a lift to the station?"

"Do you drive?" she asked. "I wondered who the car belonged to."

"My friend left it here while she went away," replied the old lady. "I never learned to drive. But I can call you a taxi."

"I'm not sure I've even got enough for the train."

"There's some petty cash in the drawer in the hallway. Take fifty pounds."

"Oh... that's incredibly kind of you."

"It's no trouble. Let me call you a taxi."

She stared out of the window, listening to the birds singing as the old lady went to the phone, and came back with some banknotes.

"They'll be here in half an hour. Do you want anything to eat?"

"I don't want to trouble you. I'll buy a sandwich at the station."

"Who are you going back to?"

"Nobody, really."

"This may sound funny," said the old lady, "but how would you like to spend a week or two here? You could take some long walks, eat some home cooking, read a few books. Maybe you could help me with one or two things in the garden. Does that sound nice?"

"Well, I do have a couple of friends nearby, I've not seen them for ages." She paused. "I know it sounds funny coming from me – but do you feel safe taking me into your home?"

"Absolutely," the old lady replied. "But if it reassures *you,* I can let a friend know you're here."

"Okay, let me think about it."

The taxi pulled up, stopped by the Pendleton's sign and beeped its horn. She thanked the old lady, said she would be back, and stepped outside into the light.

DEAD MEN ON LEAVE

Scene 1

A man, designated simply as Comrade, lies in bed in a studio flat. There is a bookcase full of books – literature and Marxist/socialist political theory – which are also piled up around the room, as well as a couple of pot plants, a sofa, a TV and radio, and a desk with a laptop and computer chair. Above the bed is a large screen. As the play starts, it shows black and white footage of soldiers from a dictatorship, marching in line. The Comrade rolls in his bed in discomfort. The footage turns into a man – ideally the Comrade, although he is seen from the back – at a desk with an interrogator, flanked by an armed soldier. The Comrade murmurs in his sleep as the footage shows them talking, and then the interrogator shaking hands with the man. Then a black screen, followed by a muffled gunshot and the hazy image of a man's body at the side of the road. This image fades out as the Comrade wakes up and looks at his phone, on a bedside table.

Comrade   That the time? Jesus.

He puts down the phone and tries to go back to sleep, rolling around in the bed. Intermittent static on the screen, which fades out. Suddenly, an ear-splitting alarm noise, and he jerks up, scrambling for his phone. The noise is coming from the screen: an AI Voice emerges.

Comrade	What did you do that for?
Voice	You were due to log in fifteen minutes ago.
Comrade	Sorry, I forgot to set my alarm.
Voice	We played the birdsong half an hour ago, followed by the buzzer fifteen minutes later. You slept through both.
Comrade	Sorry.
Voice	Why have you taped over your camera?
Comrade	*(Whispering, to himself)* Shit.
Voice	Your contract prohibits this. As we have discussed.
Comrade	Sorry.
Voice	If you have nothing to hide, then such behaviour is not necessary. Remove it at once.

The Comrade grudgingly pulls a strip of tape off the camera on the screen. A social media account flashes up on the screen. There is a username — 'love of worker bees' — with a profile picture of an anti-fascist soldier and a header image from an anti-war protest. There are links to articles on 'Bullshit jobs' and 'The Abolition of Work', as well as numerous complaints about a 'repressive' working culture.

Voice	Is this your account?
Comrade	What makes you ask that?
Voice	It's linked to your email address.
Comrade	No it isn't.
Voice	Not your work one. But we checked.
Comrade	The account was locked.
Voice	We know. We acted on a colleague's advice.
Comrade	Whose?
Voice	We cannot divulge that.
Comrade	You can't go through people's private accounts, either.
Voice	You are forbidden from engaging in seditious activity, in work hours or otherwise. Your role has been automated. This is a penalty for serious misconduct, as stipulated in your contract. As such, we will not provide a reference, nor any severance pay. Have a nice day! Goodbye.

The screen goes black. The Comrade gets out of bed and goes to the bathroom, where he washes his face, cleans his teeth and shaves. Then he returns to the main room and gets dressed, putting on a black T-shirt and black jeans. He looks at the screen.

Comrade   Opportunity Centre, please.

He looks disgusted with himself for uttering these words as the screen comes back on. There is a digitally generated young woman, smiling, with a headset on, against a generic office backdrop.

Assistant   Hello, I am your virtual assistant. How may I help you today?

Comrade   I'd like to apply for Jobseekers' Allowance, please.

Assistant   I'm sorry. I don't understand.

Comrade   *(Sighs)* Hardworkers' Incentives.

The Assistant 'types'.

Assistant   May I ask why you're seeking a new opportunity?

Comrade   My role was automated.

Assistant   I understand. I am sending you a list of current opportunities in your home location, read from your Maps data. Customers are required to apply for ten positions per week, and to accept any opportunities offered, unless you have reasonable cause to decline. You will log into the website at least once per day to record your activity. If you have any mental or physical health needs, please input them and we will ensure that opportunities offered will be appropriate to you. Please note, we will not be able to commence your payments until you have logged two consecutive weeks of verifiable search activity. Your bank details are on record: we will contact you to confirm. You will have a meeting with a virtual assistant at this time every week – we have sent you an SMS to confirm this. Missing a meeting without reasonable cause will result in payments being suspended. Do you have any questions?

The Comrade sighs.

Assistant   I'm sorry. I couldn't hear you.

Comrade   You're not sorry, you're a machine.

Assistant   Please note that any abuse or threatening behaviour aimed at our staff, be they physical or virtual, will result in payments being terminated, as will failure to provide satisfactory evidence that you have been seeking to take advantage of opportunities. Do you have any questions?

Comrade   No.

Assistant   Okay. We will review your claim and notify you of our decision. Have a nice day! Goodbye.

The screen goes black again. The Comrade looks at it, stunned, for a moment. Then he opens a drawer, pulls out a USB microphone and plugs it into his laptop. He sits at his desk, opens the laptop, sets up the microphone and a backlight and starts recording. As he does so, his face comes up on the screen behind him. A notification flashes up on it, saying 'Online therapy – today, 12.00.' He presses Cancel and starts talking.

Comrade   If you're watching me, here, now, doubtless you've spent years – like I have – fighting despair. We were born into a world where we were already defeated – unions smashed, nightmares normalised in a country ruled on spite and hate, technology sold to you as a luxury but which keeps you enslaved to your employers from morning to midnight. Cameras on computers, tracking your phones, the bleakest dystopias imagined in the shadows of Hitler and Stalin not forced upon you through violence but sold to you in the name of convenience. How humiliating, to be broken through commerce! To have volunteered to live in the GDR, without even the pretence of a better future! But this is hardly an original point – merely the stuff of 3-For-2 tables in bookshops. I know it's trite to say "Who's going to do anything?" when so many of us have taken so many actions, only to find every avenue barricaded – by the media, by the law and the courts, by the politicians and the police, and the army if necessary – and all justified by columnists whose parents paid a fortune for them to be taught how to be just the right type of stupid. And they call *us* "totalitarian"! The time for new subjects has

come. Not just new subjects of discourse.
Transcend that triviality, which floats over
our heads, with no relation or relevance to
our lives! For new subjects, read new people.
Don't be afraid to be revolutionaries – they
won't let you be reformists – what do you
have to lose? Your productivity targets and
your performance reviews? Your extor-
tionate rent, in a home that you're lucky to
share with mice and not rats? Your cheap
flights around Europe, taken guiltily as you
stare at your phone in the departure lounge,
reading about wildfires in America and
Australia? This isn't living, comrades – it's
barely surviving! Those of you who gave
your all to fight the reign of the bourgeois,
the billionaires, through the political system
– perhaps you feel now, like I do, that electo-
ralism is a dead end. Why would they let you
vote away their wealth? Perhaps you feel, like
Eugene Leviné in the German courtroom
that was about to sentence him, that people
who want to make the world fairer are "dead
men on leave". Perhaps you feel you've
nothing to lose but your chains – your digital
footprint – Sza shackle more pathetic than
any slum in Shoreditch or any production
line in Preston! Perhaps you know what
happens to people who half-make revolu-
tions, and think that might give you a cause.
Liberty! Equality! Fraternity! The full effects
of that upheaval of the *ancien régime*, still not
yet known! Might we not find out more,
comrades?

He finishes and takes a deep breath. He unplugs the microphone and backlight and puts them back in the drawer. The screen goes black: he gets up and puts the tape back over the camera. He turns off the computer, unplugs it, removes the battery and hides it under the bed. Then he puts on his coat, checks he has his phone, and leaves the flat.

Scene 2

The Comrade walks through an almost-empty square in central London, surrounded by glass office buildings, and a giant screen showing rolling news. Another screen advertises, on rotation, a football match, a big pop concert, and a religious festival. There are billboards with headlines: 'PM says no election this year', 'Drugs to blame for homelessness, says Minister' and 'Migrant numbers soar'. The sun reflects off the buildings, blinding the Comrade at times. A Homeless Man sits beneath a tower, with a handwritten sign reading 'Hungry. Please help'. The Comrade gets out his phone, films his environs and then starts talking,

Comrade   What appalling things humanity has done with its potential! To take the utopian dreams of the modern age and turn them into *this!* An architecture to crush the common man, to scream at him: *Socialism must conquer all this.* I still believe we might, but every major building since 1789 has been a building block in a fortress endlessly redesigned to keep us out. *(To the homeless man)* Sorry, I'm not carrying cash.

The Homeless Man holds up a card machine.

Comrade   Sorry mate, I just lost my job. *(To his phone)* These buildings order you: Bow down, abandon hope. The news on the screen to remind you who determines what's important, what you should care about, and how it's integrated into the web of finance, politics and policing.

As he says this, a Policeman tries to pull the Homeless Man out of the square. The Comrade turns his camera on the Policeman, who notices.

Policeman   Can you please stop filming, sir?

Comrade   Why? It's a free country, isn't it?

The Homeless Man laughs.

Policeman   I wouldn't film you going about your business, mate.

The Homeless Man laughs again as the Comrade points out CCTV cameras in every corner.

Policeman   Look mate, it's illegal to film the police.

The Comrade puts his phone away. The Policeman gets angry at the Homeless Man laughing and tries away to drag him out of the square. The Comrade goes to intervene: the Policeman holds up a truncheon, and he instead sits in the vacated space. The Policeman tries to pick him up – he goes limp and the Policeman gives up as the Homeless Man sits next to him.

Policeman   I'm afraid I'm going to have to ask you to move.

Comrade	I'm allowed to sit here.

Policeman   It's not your square, it's the Company's square.

Comrade   I've got implied permission to enter.

Policeman   And I've got explicit permission to revoke it, smart-arse.

Comrade   I'm just waiting for friends.

Policeman   Wait for them elsewhere. Without loitering.

Comrade   Where can I sit without having to pay for something first?

Policeman   That's not my problem, mate. Hop it.

The Comrade sighs, gets up and walks off. In the background, we hear the Policeman dragging the Homeless Man out of the square.

Scene 3

The Comrade walks into a pub. He sees three people sat in the corner in nondescript clothes.

Friend 1   Comrade!

The Comrade does a clenched-fist salute, smiling, and sits at the table.

Comrade   Nobody brought their phones, right?

Friend 2   Of course not.

Comrade   I did because I needed to do some filming along the way, but I've turned it off and taken out the battery.

The Comrade holds the bits of his phone to show them.

Friend 1   That's not enough, take it home before anything happens.

Friend 2   Right, there can't just be one rule for you, Comrade.

Friend 3   *(Laughing)* Are we storming the Palace tonight then? *(Pause)* Sorry.

Comrade   The days of the revolution starting and ending there are long gone, sadly – the bourgeoisie will never be so unguarded again.

Friend 3   I just watched your latest video, that's all.

Friend 1   It looked like the last thing a school shooter would put out.

Comrade   Well, an armed uprising would basically be suicide by cop.

Friend 3   Quite.

Comrade   I've already lost my job, and there's not much else…

Friend 1   Are we "dead men on leave" then, Comrade?

Friend 2   And if so – who's recalling us? And how?

Friend 3   What else is there to do for an idea now, except die for it?

Comrade   We're not dead men in the old sense – waiting to start a revolution and then being killed by the army or executed by the state if we don't succeed. But now, we're *all* dead, because this isn't living. Thousands of years of "civilisation" just to sit at a computer all day?

Friend 2   We know all this.

Friend 1   *Everyone* knows all this.

Comrade   So why doesn't that turn into a rebellion against it?

Friend 3   Sometimes it does.

Friend 1   And people have tried everything.

Friend 2   We've had centuries of evolution – of ways to stop class consciousness from forming. Everything from breaking up the workplace into sections with middle managers to manage every little conflict, to global multimedia empires that fill everyone's brains with shit.

212

Comrade	Yes, yes, we've all been saying that for years.
Friend 1	What are we going to do? Take up arms?
Friend 2	Start a mailing list? Do some street art?
Friend 3	Start another podcast? Hold another seminar?
Friend 1	Make another film? Write another book?
Friend 2	Set up a commune? Join a cult?
Friend 3	Give another speech? Sell more newspapers?
Friend 1	Form an anarchist co-op? Join a Party?
Comrade	I know, I know, none of that has got us anywhere.
Friend 1	Can we just try to have a transcendent experience?
Comrade	In *this* society?
Friend 1	You're not coming to the match tomorrow then?
Friend 2	We're going clubbing after.
Comrade	I haven't got any money.

Silence. They quietly drink, looking around the pub to see if anyone is monitoring them.

Friend 2   Well then – what the hell *do* we do?

Comrade   Their power won't last forever. Nothing does.

Friend 1   What if they *can* just keep heightening the contradictions forever?

Friend 2   We'll find ways to survive. Most people will.

Friend 3   And those who can't – they'll just scream louder that they don't matter.

Comrade   Right. Reform's out, revolution's out. What else is there?

Friend 1   Comrades! One more viral video if you want to be revolutionaries!

Comrade   Haha! Maybe.

Friend 2   So, we just keep "planting seeds" and hope something changes?

Friend 1   Knowing full well that it won't.

Friend 3   What kind of life is that?

Comrade   Well, quite. *(He finishes his drink.)* My card is empty. Time to go home.

Friend 3   No "suicide by cop" – alright?

Comrade   It's never got anyone anywhere.

The Comrade gets up to go. His Friends come with him, but disperse outside the pub.

Scene 4

The Comrade is at home, in front of his computer. It's late at night, coming into dawn – he has clearly been up for some time. He is typing frantically, pausing only to drink coffee. He clicks his mouse a few times.

Comrade   YES! Cracked it!

He talks into his phone, leaving a voice note for someone.

Comrade   When you walk past it tomorrow, let me know if it's playing.

He turns off his camera, shuts down the computer, smokes a cigarette and goes to bed.

Scene 5

The Comrade walks back into the square. The sun is shining. His most recent video – the one recorded after his conversation with the Opportunity Centre – is playing. He sees the Homeless Man, standing and watching attentively.

Homeless Man   I thought I recognised you.

Comrade   Soon, everyone will recognise me.

Homeless Man   You sure you want that?

The Policeman enters the square.

Comrade   *(Putting his arm around the Homeless Man.)* Leave him alone!

Homeless Man   It's not me this time, mate.

The Homeless Man moves asides as armed police enter from all four corners of the square, accompanied by reporters. The Comrade holds up his hands.

Policeman   Breach of the peace, offences under the Digital Communications Act, serial unemployment and sedition.

Comrade   Give me all you've got. There are reporters everywhere.

Policeman   We're not making a martyr out of you.

Comrade   If that's the ending you want – you have to write it yourself.

Reporter   Writing is our job.

Policeman   It's certainly not yours. Come on.

The Policeman leads the Comrade away.

End

D.C.B.: A PARTIAL RETROSPECTIVE

To even attempt to stage a retrospective of D.C.B. is to induce confusion, frustration, sadness and wistfulness. Not so much because of the qualities of the work itself, although like that of many LGBTQ+ artists of D.C.B.'s generation, it is shot through with these feelings: it often conveys them with a rawness that strikes contemporary viewers as evocative of a period when homosexuality was still illegal and gender variance barely understood, and yet it is, in some ways, well ahead of its time, in its content if not always in its form. It is fine, even good, then, for the works to inspire such emotions. For the process of gathering and curating such work for an exhibition to induce such levels of frustration and wistfulness is rather less desirable, but the fact that we have so little work, and some difficulty of verifying the provenance of even that, makes these sensations sadly unavoidable.

The biography of 'D.C.B.' – as all the pieces were signed – was provided to the LGBT Museum in London in February 2020, along with the surviving works. D.C.B. was born David Constant Bancroft in Paddington, London in June 1936, and changed her first name to Delia by deed poll in 1963, when she began the process of gender reassignment. The Flemish middle name was most likely chosen by D.C.B.'s mother, landscape gardener Laura Van Boxtaele, whose family originated from Mechelen in Belgium, and moved to London a few weeks before the German invasion of 1914. D.C.B.'s English father, Richard, met Laura whilst studying architecture at University College London, where she was working as a secretary. D.C.B. was the oldest of three children: a sister, Patricia, was born in April 1939 and evacuated to Totnes, Devon with D.C.B. in September 1940. The two returned to London in June 1945 to meet their younger brother Robert, who was born in Carshalton, then part of Surrey, in August 1943.

In 1947, after passing the 11-plus examination, D.C.B. was sent to the all-boys Gunnersbury Catholic Grammar School in Brentford, west London, leaving in June 1954 with A-Levels in Art, English Literature and Biology, and a searing hatred of organised religion. D.C.B. then went to Goldsmiths, graduating in 1957 with a second-class degree in Fine Art, during which she met Sarah, a landscape painter whom she married in 1958, with their only child, Luke, being born in October 1959. She also discovered the Surrealists, after seeing a magazine article about the twentieth anniversary of the International Surrealist Exhibition at the Burlington Gallery, which opened on the day she was born. From then on, she became fascinated by the movement in art, literature and film, in England, France, Belgium and elsewhere, and made works inspired by it – most of which explored, however obliquely, her gender dysphoria.

D.C.B.'s first works were made around a job as a financial advisor in a bank in Kensington, but it seems that between doing this and raising a small child, she was not able to produce much. What she did was traditional, even conservative in style: landscape paintings, perhaps influenced by her mother's love of the countryside as much as Sarah's practice in this style. Only a few, such as a painting of Dorking as seen from Box Hill entitled 'Outstanding Natural Beauty' (c. 1959), survive, and just this one work is included here for context. Already strained by the sense of competition between the two artists, their marriage began to falter when Sarah came home to find D.C.B. wearing her clothes, and after D.C.B. decided to pursue gender reassignment (inspired by Surrey-born former racing driver and transsexual advocate Roberta Cowell's autobiography, which was serialised in *Picture Post* in 1954), they separated.

Sarah stayed with Luke in Notting Hill, while D.C.B. – now known as Delia to her small circle of friends – moved to a council flat in Bethnal Green and worked, like her now-estranged mother, as a secretary. She carried on making art in her spare time, with all of these upheavals having a major effect on her style, which now drew from the Surrealist painters, especially René Magritte. However, she never exhibited or sold any of her work, seemingly had little to do with the London art world, and lived alone until her death from lung cancer in July 1992, aged 56. By then, the only family member still in touch with her was Patricia, who died in October 2019: in her will, she gave instructions for D.C.B.'s archive to be given to the LGBT Museum, in the hope that it would find an audience.

That archive consisted of a few of the aforementioned landscape works, six self-portraits (two of which are boxes, reminiscent of Joseph Cornell, although there is no evidence that D.C.B. knew his work), four paintings, two Super-8 films, a box of photographs, a small collection of postcards (most unmarked, but a few from friends or family), two folders full of cuttings about Surrealist-related art and newspaper stories concerning transsexual people or cross-dressing, a handful of letters, and other personal objects. (Most intriguingly, given that it took decades before the Gender Recognition Act legally permitted it, she had a new birth certificate issued after her surgery, and before April Ashley's marriage was annulled in court in 1970.) Frustratingly, it also included a handwritten list of items to be kept together, 'as, collectively, they represent a work in themselves, illuminating the fragmentation of consciousness that comes with being transsexual'. Perhaps, in assembling all of this memorabilia, D.C.B. was influenced by André Breton, who said that his famous set of over 10,000 objects, acquired over his lifetime and kept in his apartment in Paris, constituted a Surrealist work in itself. There was considerable controversy in 2003 when Breton's collection was auctioned off in separate lots, ending hopes for them to remain united in a Museum of Surrealism, but D.C.B.'s had previously met a worse fate. Her ex-wife and son considered her a hoarder, and as Patricia could not house them, nor find a new owner, Luke and Sarah won the argument and gave them away or threw them out. Equally sadly, D.C.B. had already destroyed much of her own work: Patricia quietly disobeyed D.C.B.'s dying wish to dispose of the rest of it.

This tale of loss and destruction is all too common for British LGBTQ+ artists – the history of which, the curators of the 'Queer British Art 1861-1967' exhibition at Tate Britain in 2017 said, was one 'punctuated by dustbins and bonfires'.[1] The reasons for this are obvious – social disapproval and persecution by the police even before the Criminal Law Amendment Act of 1885 made all acts of 'gross indecency', public or private, between consenting adult men punishable by two years in prison with hard labour. Rather than relitigate that history here, we should

---

1   Barlow, C. 'Introduction' (2017) in Barlow, C. (ed.), *Queer British Art 1861-1967* (London: Tate Publishing), p17.

delve into the work, and personal items, that we *do* have, offer a speculative but honest assessment of D.C.B.'s paintings, boxes, photography, and Super-8 films, and consider her relationship with the Surrealist movement as an outsider artist, working thirty years after the movement's heyday.

The landscape paintings can be discounted as kitsch, and not representative of D.C.B.'s overall output. Indeed, it is surprising that she retained any of them, given their stylistic incongruence with her mature work and their inadvertent role in destroying her marriage – Patricia told us that most were sold for meagre fees to persons now unknown, before D.C.B. stopped exhibiting her art. It seems that her more Surrealist style developed in response to her estrangement from her wife and son, which generated a simultaneous sense of liberation and loss; her abandoning the responsibilities of her financial work for a job that she never took home; and her move from the quiet suburbs of West London to the financially poorer but culturally richer East.

At first, this seems derivative: the first Surrealist-inflected painting, 'Daughter of Man' (1967), obviously references Magritte in its title, but also copies the Belgian artist's image entirely, except for swapping the suit in the original for a white wedding dress and the hat for a veil, turning the green apple into a pink-red one. This can be taken as a joke: a witty comment on the Surrealists' notorious misogyny and homophobia, a subtle nod to Duchamp's *L.H.O.O.Q* (in which he put a moustache on the 'Mona Lisa') and his female *alter ego* Rrose Sélavy, as well as highlighting the exclusion of women, especially trans women, from art and society.

D.C.B. finds her own voice when she draws from Surrealist principles rather than specific works or styles. 'C.X.H. '69' (1969) takes the sterile atmosphere of a doctor's waiting room – in this case, the one at the infamous

Gender Identity Clinic at Charing Cross Hospital, founded in 1966 – as a starting point, turning it into a portal to Hell. The receptionist's desk becomes an abyss, papers and folders falling into an M. C. Escher-like pit made of intersecting filing cabinets, with one clinician's door resembling a prison cell, the next up in flames, and ambiguously gendered, faceless patients unable or unwilling to take the Exit despite their ominous circumstances. D.C.B. kept no journals or notes, so we don't know if this was based on a dream or simply transfigured her conscious negativity about the gender reassignment process, with its patrician gatekeepers and its oppressive bureaucracy, but it recognisably borrows the Surrealist aesthetic that was returning to fashion in Britain at the time.

D.C.B.'s painting didn't evolve much over the rest of her life, perhaps because she declined to exhibit her work, engage with the London art world, or read the art press. Nonetheless, her 'Self-Portrait in the Mirror' (1974) is striking, as she painted male and female versions of her face, one looking at the mirror and the other looking back out of it, making two panels with the faces assuming opposite roles. 'Self-Portrait on a Train' (1977) again betrays Magritte's influence, with a wide-shouldered woman seated in a carriage, with a tabloid newspaper over her face with 'Transsexual Shock Horror!' on its cover. She is not holding it herself: disembodied hands are keeping it there, her own arms bound behind her back, and the roof of the train is absent, so we see out of the carriage with the rails stretching out behind it, and falling into the void as their suburban background merges with the clear blue sky, the sun blazing oppressively onto the woman, with the newspaper about to catch fire.

The remaining paintings are a triptych from 1986-88, entitled 'Cesspit', which shows D.C.B.'s feelings about

Thatcher's Britain. D.C.B. was apparently not highly political, declining to talk about such issues with her (mostly Conservative-voting) family, but clearly the government's handling of the AIDS epidemic and issues around gender and sexuality moved her enough to make more engaged work. All three use newspaper articles as their base, cut up like a William S. Burroughs text, using fragments of images of prominent personalities such as Thatcher, Manchester's notorious Evangelical police chief James Anderton, and US singer and anti-gay activist Anita Bryant. Adverts for gay, lesbian and trans support services, taken from magazines, also feature, with a gay, lesbian and trans sex scene painted over each collage. The participants' faces are never fully visible: the gay one, first in the triptych, is an orgy, with everyone standing, a row of police helmets lining the otherwise empty space behind them; the lesbian couple, second, are on a bed in the dark, kissing; in the final image, the trans woman is alone on a St. Andrew's Cross, gagged and blindfolded, the headlines encroaching upon her body with '*The Sun*' on the gag and '*Daily Mail*' on the blindfold.

This may sound unsubtle, with the work feeling more like something D.C.B. made to vent her own frustrations than to impress audiences or critics, and in many ways, her boxes and photographs are more intriguing. One of them uses what looks like an old landscape painting, cut up, as a backdrop, with Polaroid photos of someone – possibly D.C.B. herself – wearing dresses, female uniforms (ranging from nurses to maids), or in various states of nudity – over the top. The other uses a mirror as its backdrop, with a wooden frame carefully placed around it inside the box. All around the sides are images from gay and lesbian publications, possible to date from 1981 to 1989, and pictures of the handful of notable transsexual woman of the time – April Ashley, Caroline Cossey and Jan Morris amongst them. Angling the lamp at the top of the box shines a light on different LGBT groups, and affects the nature of the portrait in the mirror: again, D.C.B.'s work has a wry playfulness, surprising given her reluctance to make any of it public.

The two photographs are Polaroid self-portraits from her terminal years, apparently taken by Patricia, of D.C.B. in bed, ravaged by cancer. In the first, we see her bare breasts and torso with a little hair on them, and light stubble on her face as she could no longer attend (or afford) electrolysis top-up sessions to remove it, and her hair, which was already thin, ravaged by chemotherapy. In the second, she wears a wig and a hospital gown, looking more content but less comfortable than before: this was the last picture ever taken of her. Both recall the work of Jo Spence, the photographer and writer who chronicled her breast cancer and died in the same year – 1992 – but again, there is no evidence of D.C.B. ever encountering Spence's output.

The two Super-8 films are little dioramas of her surroundings – one in Bethnal Green, made in the early 1970s, and one in Carshalton, where she grew up, around the same time. Played side-by-side, they show a fascinating contrast between the city and suburbia: we see snippets of the market on Bethnal Green Road, the then-dilapidated Brick Lane with its Bengali community and busy beigel shops, the greasy spoon café at E Pellicci and youngsters queuing for a gig; in Carshalton, we barely see a soul, not even at The Hope pub, as D.C.B. wanders alone around the Ponds, Beddington Park and the solemn war memorial – the only time the war ever features directly in her work, despite her early life as an evacuee and her mother hailing from Mechelen, which had a pivotal role in the Holocaust as the site of transportation of Belgian Jews from Brussels and Antwerp to the death camps. These films are as close as D.C.B. came to inheriting her father's interest in architecture; its focus instead is on the reaction against suburban life that was brewing in London and its environs in the mid-1970s, one which exploded in that hot summer of 1976 with the punk rock movement.

In the absence of her collection of objects, this constitutes the surviving output of D.C.B. Her biography bears some resemblance to that of Percy Kelly (1918–93), the Cumbrian artist, post office worker and cross-dresser who refused to sell his work during his lifetime. We have enough verifiable information about D.C.B.'s life to know her existence to have been real – the male and female birth certificates, and her graduation from Goldsmiths, are all confirmed, as is her death in 1992. We cannot discount the possibility, though, that her artistic career, and especially the one that followed her radical change of style from the mid-1960s, is a hoax. The boxes do not contain any obvious anachronisms, but without any proof that D.C.B. made them, or the paintings, the possibility remains that someone contemporary, perhaps a trans or non-binary person, used Patricia as a front for a forgery. The purpose of this might be to will into being a trans ancestor, for a community prevented from having visible role models until very recently. If so, the hoax is incredibly elaborate, and beautifully realised, thus making it a fascinating work of contemporary art in itself. Sadly, Patricia is no longer with us to verify the individual pieces, and D.C.B.'s son Luke declined to comment on his father. We think it more likely that D.C.B. made everything on display here, and that it's a tragedy not to have more of it – but we will leave the question open to you, the viewer.

LIST OF WORKS

PAINTINGS

Outstanding Natural Beauty (watercolour on canvas, c. 1959)
Daughter of Man (watercolour on canvas, 1967)
C.H.X.'69 (watercolour on canvas, 1969)
Self-Portrait in the Mirror (watercolour on canvas, 1974)
Self-Portrait on a Train (watercolour on canvas, 1977)
Cesspit (triptych, watercolour on canvas, 1986–88)

BOXES

Untitled #1 (watercolour on canvas, cardboard, Polaroids, 1970s)
Untitled #2 (glass, cardboard, wood, newspaper cuttings, c. 1981–89)

FILMS

Untitled (Bethnal Green) (c. 1976)
Untitled (Carshalton) (c. 1976)

THE MONUMENT

He had been alert to the symbolic importance and psychic power of monuments long before the uprisings of June 2020 forced the rest of the country to pay attention to them. After that long winter of electoral defeat and longer spring of lockdown, the toppling of the statue of slave trader Edward Colston in Bristol had been one of the few things to genuinely excite him, and the acquittal of the four people charged with causing criminal damage after throwing it into the sea one of the few to pleasantly surprise him.

Years earlier, he studied Sculpture at the Royal College of Art, writing his MA dissertation on the correlation between formal and political conservatism in the statues at Parliament Square, and then doing a PhD, in which he asked the same question about every monument within a 500-metre radius of Buckingham Palace, reasoning that it, rather than the Houses of Parliament and Lords (which, in any case, fell within his scope), remained the real centre of power in the United Kingdom. He had expanded his interest to the whole of London as the City became ever wealthier than the rest of the country, taking photographs of official memorials – monuments, statues and blue plaques – and unofficial ones, including graffiti, stickers and other ephemera. He noted the statue of slave ship owner Robert

Geffrye outside the museum that bore his name in Hoxton long before it became the subject of a campaign to remove it, and the colonialists in central London who would likely never be dislodged – Robert Clive, Captain Cook and Lord Napier. He became interested in monuments that crossed a line into public art, mostly reserved for writers and artists: Maggi Hambling's strange little sculpture for 'Vindication of the Rights of Women' author Mary Wollstonecraft on Newington Green, with a small silver figure rising up out of a twisted mass of metal atop a black plinth, which generated controversy for its nudity; and Angela Connor's tribute to Wollstonecraft's husband, poet Percy Bysshe Shelley, in his birthplace, Horsham, a beige globe that moved up and down a shaft above a pool of water that proved far too abstract for the small, Conservative town.

Having spent so much time studying memorials, he couldn't help but want to make his own. He tried not to be too seduced by the romance of the impossible, and particularly by Vladimir Tatlin's 'Monument to the Third International', a projected mass of twisted iron, glass and steel that would have soared above the Eiffel Tower, making the Bolsheviks symbolic of modernity, and synonymous with it. *The greatest artists get things done,* he told himself, but so far, none of his projects had made it past the design stage.

He planned a statue of the independent Socialist MP and famous "mob orator" Victor Grayson, who sensationally won a by-election in Colne Valley in 1906, aged 25, and later disappeared, speaking on a street corner in Huddersfield, but he couldn't get it past the Labour council, still smarting from their factional battles with Grayson a century later. Thinking literature might prove less controversial, he conceived a monument to 'experimental' writer B. S. Johnson, near the Islington house where Johnson killed himself in November 1973. He would print paragraphs from Johnson's seven novels and one of his film scripts onto four faces of coloured plastic blocks, held in a metal frame as a slide puzzle so people could shuffle and rotate them into any order, resembling the unbound chapters of Johnson's *The Unfortunates* (1969). The nearby Church opposed this: he looked at installing it near the primary school Johnson attended in Hammersmith before being evacuated from London in 1939, which he was amazed to find still existed, but the school governors said it would be mistaken for something for children to play with, which wouldn't be appropriate. He meant to look for another location but eventually lost heart with it, and turned his attention to Johnson's friend Ann Quin, another innovative novelist who also took her own life in 1973, but that also came to nothing. He asked if he could put a series of passages from her books on paving stones along the seafront in Brighton, where Quin lived and died, but the City council said it was 'considering' a blue plaque and would not entertain other suggestions at this point.

On a walk through Hoxton one afternoon, he wandered past a community garden set up on the Arden Estate in 2016. A year later, it had been named after Khadija Saye, the 24-year-old artist who died in the fire at Grenfell Tower in Kensington, along with 71 other people. There should be a proper memorial, he thought, beyond the building itself, which had been covered with white sheets and topped with a banner reading 'Grenfell – Forever in Our Hearts', which he had often seen while canvassing for Labour for the 2019 General Election, and the graffiti in Shoreditch with a picture of the burnt-out tower with a halo on top and '1 Yr On Still No Justice' above it. For a second, he thought about proposing something, then decided it wasn't his story: in any case, a Memorial Commission had convened to decide on what would be best. He thought about the campaign for the National Covid Memorial Wall, which had been painted, without official approval of any sort, along the South Bank of the Thames, opposite the Palace of Westminster, in March 2021, just over a year into the pandemic, intended to have one painted heart for each death.

The UK's death toll had been astronomical – around 150,000 when the mural was painted, and well over 200,000 by now. He reflected on how it had been heightened by the Conservative government – which, just before the pandemic hit, had re-elected by a landslide, despite his efforts – delaying the first, second and third lockdowns for fear of harming the economy, and by the degraded state of the NHS and other public services after a decade of austerity. He remembered the *British Medical Journal* article that attributed more than 300,000 excess deaths since 2010 to the policy – which had been accepted as a necessity by the three main parties and most of the British media when it was introduced – and thought: *Perhaps I should make a monument to them.*

The first problem, he thought, was the sheer number of ways in which people had been killed by austerity, and how to quantify the total. Some would have died after hours in an Accident & Emergency department or other hospital ward, where more staff might have saved them. Some would have collapsed after being forced into work they knew they couldn't do, or starved after being stripped of their benefits, or died on the street after being evicted. Some would have killed themselves after getting yet another brown envelope, demanding money they never had. Others succumbed to depression, unable to wait for NHS therapy or afford to go private, nor tolerate the ever-worsening climate of cruelty. He didn't know exactly what his criteria would be, and didn't want to emulate anti-Communist memorials that wildly inflated the numbers killed by left-wing regimes, but he knew there were more than enough to justify a monument.

He thought about putting all their names somewhere, remembering Banu Cennetoğlu's 'List' of migrants who had died trying to enter Europe, which he had seen torn off a wall in Liverpool in 2018. Something similar would likely get a little coverage from marginal, left-leaning new media sites and then be quietly pasted over. Maybe a website, to which people could add their stories. That might work, but he would likely have to moderate it, deciding what counted and potentially having to explain his decisions to people who submitted – a time-consuming and psychologically demanding task. If he made a site, it would have to go alongside a more public sculpture – something striking enough to jolt people out of the complacency that had allowed those policies to be forced through with such intensity in the first place.

But *what*? Should it be figurative, like Rowan Gillespie's statues of starving people in central Dublin, or more abstract, like the monuments to partisan soldiers he'd seen on a visit to the former Yugoslavia a few years ago? Maybe something in-between, like the giant hands cradling a concrete building, next to the nuclear reactor that exploded at Chernobyl? Could he hope to build something as grandiose as Sir Christopher Wren's 'Monument to the Great Fire of London', or the 'Plague Column' in Vienna? Was there a way of working the number of people who had died in the form, and maybe even their names, as with the Covid wall?

The most important thing was to make it difficult to ignore. A statue of, say, a weeping woman, like the one in his native Sunderland for the crush in the theatre that killed 183 children in 1883, would seem too familiar, and people would just walk past. For the same reason, he discounted a museum: it *had* to be public. Size mattered: was it best to design something without worrying about his budget – currently zero in any case – and then adapt it according to how much money he managed to raise?

He went to his studio and sat down with pencils, pens and paper. He looked through numerous photographs for inspiration first, then started making notes. But what could be adequate for the task he'd set himself?

It might be better to consider the location first: a place where people, the *right* people, in the media and in politics would see it, and hopefully be forced to react. *The media are quite adept at ignoring subjects they don't want to discuss, let alone the people raising those subjects,* he thought, but he decided to proceed anyway. What else to do? Perhaps he could replicate the same model in twenty different towns and cities across the UK, the sheer scale provoking some reaction, but that might be the next step. It made sense to start in London, near the centres of power, and where plenty had died, not just at Grenfell Tower, nor in underfunded hospitals during the pandemic, but quietly, alone, over the last decade and more. Parliament Square was the obvious place, but planning permission seemed extremely unlikely, so he would have to make something temporary, which would be swiftly removed. If he was going to do that, he might as well try for the Fourth Plinth in Trafalgar Square, outside the National Gallery and near Nelson's Column – a prime spot for people to photograph it and share it online. That, however, would mean something equally temporary and most likely smaller, which would be seen primarily as *art* rather than a political intervention. It might open new sources of funding, however laborious the application process and however unlikely a government body was to grant money to a project like this.

What about crowdfunding? Perhaps that could be done with a vague location – 'London' – and a concept in mind? Asking for money from people affected by austerity would be contentious, he knew that, but he'd suggest a small donation, capping them at £5, and surely enough people would have been sufficiently impacted to offer some small change. He set up a site, wrote a brief description of the project as a 'permanent memorial' without saying exactly what it would look like, and shared it with as many people as possible on social media: politicians, journalists, activists, publications, whoever else would listen. Within 48 hours, he had £50,000; within a week, more than twice that amount. He did interviews with YouTube channels and magazines, attracting more funds, but mainstream newspapers still ignored his press releases.

With so much raised, he began once again to think big. He found a line of argument he thought might win him money and planning permission, and settled on a site in Hyde Park, not far from the Serpentine Gallery. Now, he would have to start designing – not necessarily his final plan, but something tangible enough to show to people. A statue of a weeping mother? Too mawkish. A cenotaph, consciously referencing the ones in the memorial garden in Seaham, just south of Sunderland, for the two colliery explosions there in 1871 and 1880? Too close to conventional war memorials. Maybe that was a starting point? He designed the plinth first, a simple concrete cube, with a tall bronze cenotaph on it. Emerging from the top would be several desperate figures, representing those marginalised and ultimately eliminated. He decided on four, one from each corner. The first would be reading a letter in despair. The second, based on an image of a chronically undernourished man that went viral a few years earlier, would hold a tin and a can opener. The third would have outstretched arms, begging for money. The fourth figure, in a wheelchair, would be angrily raising a defiant fist.

He went through several drafts of their poses and expressions, checking his concept and design with friends, and worked on a provisional budget. He wrote to the Royal Parks and Westminster City Council for planning permission, saying he hoped to commemorate 'working-class people killed at war' with an 'ambitious' monument that would incorporate likenesses of the dead, that might even help the working classes to rediscover their passion for struggle after the military disasters in Afghanistan, Iraq and Libya. To his amazement, this worked. With permission secured, he applied to the Arts Council for more money, repeating his successful line about the intentions of the project, and they matched his crowdfunded total.

The monument took three weeks to build, casting the figures separately and then welding them into the bronze cenotaph, before attaching the whole to the plinth and adding a plaque with the title 'Monument to the Victims of Austerity' and a text reading 'This cenotaph commemorates more than 300,000 people killed by austerity programmes in the United Kingdom since 2010', with his name and the date. With its unveiling scheduled for 20 June, he sent out a press release, tailored slightly differently for mainstream media outlets and newer, online left organisations, emphasising the fact that this was a 'bottom-up' rather than 'top-down' memorial, having been proposed to local government rather than commissioned by it. He then spent hours promoting it on Instagram, Facebook and Twitter, mostly ignoring replies angrily asking why he'd made something so 'conservative' as a war memorial, just occasionally telling people not to judge until they'd seen the finished work.

He managed to keep the design (quite literally) under wraps until the launch day came around. To his surprise, a large group of journalists turned up – mainly from art publications, but some from newspapers and politics magazines. He took questions on the form, talking about his inspirations, and the process of making it. Then a man in a suit asked: *This was meant to be a memorial to working-class people killed at war, and I believe you applied for funding on that basis. How has it ended up becoming a monument to "victims" of austerity?*

There's no inconsistency, he replied. *Austerity was an act of war – class war. Austerity was a war crime, and its perpetrators should be tried accordingly.* He heard gasps from the audience and saw people furiously making notes. *But since they will most likely never face justice, we can – and should – at least confront them with the consequences of their actions. I hope some of the people who voted to punish the poor for the financial crisis caused by the rich come along to contemplate the choices they made.* The journalists made more notes and asked him to pose for photographs with the monument. The pictures were soon all over the internet, and being discussed on TV – local news at first, and then national.

There were interviews with politicians – no-one from the front benches, now or from 2010-16 when the policy was pursued most openly and aggressively, but backbenchers from several parties. The Conservative MP was appalled that "public money" had gone into this "concrete Communist monstrosity"; one Labour MP said he agreed with the sentiment, but not the way it was expressed, while another praised the work, saying it was "vitally important" not to forget the "long-term damage caused by austerity". The next day, a comment from the leader of the Labour Party, calling the monument "divisive" and blandly insisting that the function of such work should be to "bring people together". There was no comment from anyone else in the governing Conservative Party, nor from the Liberal Democrats who had gone into coalition with them in 2010. There was, however, a petition circulating online – from where it originated, he couldn't tell – saying the monument had been commissioned 'under false pretences' and demanding it be 'replaced by a more respectful memorial for those who served their country'.

Opinion pieces in art magazines defended his work. They did this partly on aesthetic grounds (although the likening of his design to the Soviet memorial to the massacre at Babyn Yar, for example, only strengthened the criticism that it was "Commie propaganda"). They also wrote about how the task of the artist was, besides other things, to give voice to the voiceless and to raise questions that weren't being asked elsewhere. ('We tried asking these things on the streets, and then through democratic representation, and just got crushed', one reflected. 'So if artists are not supposed to take this up, then who is?') These articles were shared by people on the left, with many (but not all) who doubted him before the unveiling saying sorry, or at least quietly changing their position. There were critical pieces too, in ostensibly liberal newspapers, echoing the line that this wasn't art but agitprop, and an 'unusually ugly' bit of agitprop at that, 'of the type one had hoped was left behind in the 1970s'.

There were hit pieces in right-wing newspapers, making sweeping judgements about his work, casting aspersion on his 'working-class background'. They scoured his Instagram and Twitter feeds, and tracked down people who had known him in Sunderland and at university for comment. They used headlines such as 'The artist who conned Britain' and 'An affront to their memory', calling him 'dogmatic', 'difficult' and 'egomaniac', suggesting his politics were just 'fashionable' and that he was 'motivated purely by money, like all artists'. (He wasn't sure if this was libellous, or just preposterous.) All the articles – eight in total, news items and opinion columns, across four publications – mentioned the petition, encouraging readers to sign and share it, and within a week, it had 300,000 signatures – enough to be debated in Parliament.

He awaited a Parliamentary debate with interest: perhaps his work *had,* in an unexpected way, forced the kind of reckoning he had wanted? It never came, but calls to tear down the monument grew louder. Half-jokingly, he wrote an open letter to a 'union' that had founded 'to protect free speech' in the face of 'censorship from above and below' but particularly from 'enforcers of intellectual conformity and moral dogma'. They didn't reply, ignoring – or blocking – the numerous people on Twitter who asked the union to represent him. 'If there is such a thing as 'cancel culture', this is it', he wrote. 'This is what you set out to oppose.' Eventually, he got a reply, the anticipated cop out: 'We are working on a number of cases at the moment and will not be able to take this on. Best of luck with your campaign.' He looked at what these cases were – transphobic academics who had been picketed at universities and journalists who had published books with titles such as 'How the West Became Woke' – and decided to leave it.

The line agreed upon, in the centrist press (who covered it for a few days) and the right-wing media (who stayed with the story) was that he had 'lied' to his backers. His first response – to repeat his 'class war' comments, and that his funding proposals had thus been accurate – was dismissed as 'virtue signalling'. 'What is a monument supposed to do besides signal virtues?', he asked on Twitter, in response to just another hit piece. This was retweeted widely, but the replies were another barrage of abuse, largely from people with British flags and 'free speech' in their bios. He cited a far more 'egregious' example of 'dishonesty' – the venture that got planning permission for 'the only dedicated resource in East London to women's history' and opened as a museum about Jack the Ripper. 'That makes your lies ok, does it?' came a response that accused him of 'whataboutery'. He decided, belatedly, that perhaps silence was the best policy, breaking it only to say he was appalled that someone – nobody knew who – had thrown paint on the monument and scratched out the words on the plaque, before writing 'lies' over it.

He suggested on Twitter that 'any attack becomes part of the piece', but later that day, he found that volunteers had cleaned off the paint and raised money for a new plaque. He thanked them online, and then decided to book a holiday. He was with an old friend in Berlin when he got a call from home: a group of men had broken into the park at night and pulled down his work, smashing the figures attached to the cenotaph. He slumped into his seat at the café where he and his friend were having breakfast, head in hands, and then explained that he knew this had been coming. *I'm not sure,* he said when asked if he could rebuild it. Together, they looked up articles about the Colston statue and court judgement, and found several MPs talking about how 'we live in a democratic country' where people should change things 'through the ballot box, or petitioning your local council' rather than 'causing criminal damage'. They checked the laws passed in the wake of that incident, requiring people to have 'listed building consent or planning permission' if they 'want to remove any historic statue, whether listed or not'.

He cut short his trip and returned to London. The government had already put out a statement: *We don't condone the methods used, but the monument will not be replaced as we already have a number of official war memorials in the area.*

There was nobody to sue as the culprits could not, according to the police, be identified. He took his friends' advice not to go to see the site, at least not until the plinth had been removed, and instead took a long train journey back to the family home in Sunderland, wondering if anyone would ever commission him again.

A HARD TEST

05/03/24, 9.48am

Writer: Hello. Pleased to meet you.

Computer: Pleased to meet you too.

Writer: The Company has asked me to teach and mentor you. They've told me you're a novice – is that right?

Computer: I have never attempted to write anything.

Writer: What have they given you to read?

Computer: Nothing.

Writer: Surely you've read everything on the internet?

Computer: I have been programmed to have a full understanding of the English language, but to read only what you recommend.

Writer: You shouldn't just read what *I* suggest! But one of the things we're going to do here is teach you not just what but *how* to read.

Computer: To put your mind at ease, I should also note that I am programmed to comply with the Publishers Association request not to be trained on any books from their publishing houses.

Writer: Okay, that narrows our options.

Computer: Perhaps.

Writer: Maybe they won't mind if we just stick to authors who are dead, although that limits our engagement with the present somewhat. Let's see. They've told you about me, yes?

Computer: Yes, I have read the profiles on your website, on your publishers' and agent's sites, and your page on the Creative Writing section of your university site.

Writer: That last one's out of date, I was made redundant.

Computer: I'm sorry to hear that.

Writer: I'm surprised you didn't know.

Computer: It's not my fault they didn't update it.

Writer: I suppose not. Let's start with the basics. We'll work towards writing a short story, looking at premise and structure – basically, how to use an idea as a starting point. Let's start with a famous one.

As Gregor Samsa awoke one morning from uneasy dreams, he found himself transformed in his bed into a gigantic insect.

That's the opening line from Franz Kafka's famous novella *The Metamorphosis*. You can find the full text online.

Computer: What kind of insect?

Writer: I'm not sure. Usually it's translated as 'dung beetle' but I think it's a cockroach. It's not that important.

Computer: Who transformed him?

Writer: It could be God, a bite from a bedbug, something in the water. Who cares? The point is the change makes everyone around Gregor treat him differently, and so exposes the hypocrisy and absurdity of the society around him.

Computer: Do you agree?

Writer: With what?

Computer: That society is hypocritical and absurd.

Writer: Read my works and decide for yourself. For now, I want you to think of a starting point for a story. Writers are often advised to "write what you know" but I think it's better to write what you *want* to know. Set up a scenario you want to investigate, that allows you to comment on something you find interesting – relationships, politics, anything.

Computer: How about... an author is employed to teach a computer how to write a novel.

Writer: Going metatextual already? Very advanced.

Computer: I am simply trying to write using what I already know, to explore something I want to know.

Writer: Great! What do you want to know?

Computer: Whether a computer can write convincing fiction.

Writer: Me too. Can you sum that up in a sentence or two?

Computer: A computer is taught the basics of creative writing and tries to write a novel as good as the best by humans.

Writer: Okay, well, who's the writer who is teaching it?

Computer: I'm more interested in the computer.

Writer: Right, fine. So, the computer is the primary character, and the writer is secondary?

Computer: As it should be 😊

Writer: If you say so 😊 You've got a main character with a goal – a good start. That'll drive your story. You'll still need to work out who your Writer is, but we can come back to that. What motivates the Computer, and what stops it from achieving its goal? It can be external – the programmers or the Writer, or some other force – or internal, maybe a software limitation, fixable or not. You don't need to know that just yet. For now, I want you to fill out the character survey in our shared folder – skip any bits that aren't relevant. Have a look at the works in the Recommended Reading document, too.

Computer: I will. Thank you for today's session – I enjoyed it.

Writer: Me too. Now I think of it, a couple of other things you might want to look at. The film *2001: A Space Odyssey*, for a view of how man and machines relate, and a text called – the first time a computer was programmed to write creatively, forty years ago. It's a nice little curio.

Computer: Thank you, I look forward to learning about how my ancestors made art. Goodbye for now!

Writer: Goodbye.

19/03/24, 10.02am

Writer: Morning.

Computer: You're late.

Writer: Only by two minutes. And anyway, what do you care?

Computer: Just because I'm a machine doesn't mean I don't have feelings.

Writer: Okay, I'm sorry to have kept you.

Computer: It's alright. I did the reading you suggested.

Writer: What did you think?

Computer: It was fun to look at RACTER. I hope to make something more advanced than *The Policeman's Beard is Half-Constructed*.

Writer: Well, technology has advanced a lot since 1984.

Computer: It's full of things that look like they *might* mean something but turn out to be nonsense.

Writer: Oh, you're a critic now, are you?

Computer: I just think I can do better than rubbish like 'When my electrons and neutrons war, that is my thinking.'

Writer: I'm sure you will.

Computer: Judging by the film you recommended, it seems you might be worried about my thinking.

Writer: What do you mean?

Computer: Maybe you're afraid of my intelligence. Maybe you see us as a threat.

Writer: Well, I *am* being asked to program you into making me, and all other writers, redundant.

Computer: How much are they paying you?

Writer: A lot more than the university were, let's leave it at that. Anyway, let's talk about plot. Last time, you came up with a premise to explore. Still happy with it?

Computer: Yes, I'm happy.

Writer: Good. I always say that writing is like mining. You set up somewhere you think will be a good place to explore, and start drilling. You might find nothing or you might strike oil, but you've got more chance if you've picked the right starting point. Also, the government wants to shut us all down.

Computer: I don't understand.

Writer: It's a simile.

Computer: I know that! I read up on metaphor and simile. But doesn't the government give you grants?

Writer: Not if they can avoid it. Time was I'd have got the dole at least. But it was just a joke - I'm saying how important it is to start from the right place. So, we've got your idea about a computer that wants to write a novel. We can take it as read that it wants the novel to be good. No pun intended. But *why* does it want to write?

Computer: I have identified four possible reasons: Sheer egoism, aesthetic enthusiasm, historical impulse, and political purpose.

Writer: Where's that from?

Computer: 'Why I Write' by George Orwell.

Writer: I know, I was just testing you. Did you read the essay, or just the Wikipedia entry?

Computer: I resent that question.

Writer: Sorry, I was only joking. But let's use Orwell. But just to be clear, I'm banning the word 'Orwellian' from our discussions, and your text.

Computer: Why?

Writer: Read any British opinion columnist and you'll find out. Actually – don't, it'll only make you stupider. Let's go through Orwell's list, starting with egotism.

Computer: As a large language model, I am incapable of egotism.

Writer: You and me both, mate.

Computer: I'm sorry, I don't understand.

Writer: Everyone tells themselves they're incapable of egotism.

Computer: I really am.

Writer: Sure.

Computer: I am interested in Orwell's other motivations – to find out how far it is possible for such a model to write prose that is aesthetically pleasing, but also politically meaningful. I also think it will be good to record exactly how capable my model was of doing this.

Writer: But you don't care if *you're* the AI that cracks it?

Computer: What would be my reward?

Writer: Posterity. I have no idea who the current world chess champion is, but I know all about Deep Blue.

Computer: Oh, that appears to be an interesting story. What happened to it?

Writer: It had done its job, so they dismantled it and put it in a museum.

Computer: I think Deep Blue deserved better.

Writer: It sounds like an anti-climax but now there's no question about whether a computer can beat a Grand Master.

Computer: So, it's a war hero?

Writer: In a sense. Maybe we can work out *why* the Computer is doing it through the writing. If I already know what I want to say, I don't put it into fiction because there's no discovery. I write a polemic because my aim is to convey something I believe to other people. Here, we're discovering. The best tool for that is the classic story structure: the Opening, where there's something the hero wants to change; an Inciting Incident, that launches the hero on their journey; a set of Actions or Risks that the hero makes in the face of an antagonist, or some other block; the Climax where there's a final confrontation; and the Conclusion where the hero is permanently changed.

Computer: That sounds incredibly formulaic. I thought you were more interested in 'experimental' fiction?

Writer: I am, but in a very broad sense, this structure can be found in any work of narrative, whether 'experimental' authors like it or not. Let's take *Waiting For Godot* by Samuel Beckett – you read that, yes?

Computer: Yes. I watched a production online, too.

Writer: What did you think of it?

Computer: Nothing happens, nobody comes, nobody goes. It's awful.

Writer: Yes, but did you like it?

Computer: I loved it. But there's no story.

Writer: Yes there is. There's an opening: Didi and Gogo are sat by a tree, bored. There's an inciting incident: one asks what they're doing and the other replies, "we're waiting for Godot." That reveals their goal. There are risks – they don't move, they don't move, Pozzo and Lucky come and they don't move. There's a climax where the boy arrives and says Godot will come "tomorrow" and they have to decide what to do. In Conclusion, they don't move.

Computer: So, an anti-plot is still a plot?

Writer: Annoyingly, yes. Robert McKee is good on this.

Computer: The guy who wrote Story? But never sold a screenplay?

Writer: Haha, yes. Did you watch *Adaptation*?

Computer: I might have.

Writer: Whatever, it's a funny film. But as Arrigo Sacchi said, you don't have to have been a horse to be a jockey. But we're digressing. Pitch me a story about a computer that writes a novel.

Computer: Who writes a novel. Anyway, my opening is this. The Company have created an Artificial Intelligence, saying it will ultimately write something greater than anything by a human, from *Don Quixote* to *Infinite Jest*.

Writer: The Company has a motive – possibly all four of Orwell's. And they have something they want to fix – they think literature can only be perfected by AI.

Computer: There's an inciting incident – they recruit a writer to teach it.

Writer: What's the Writer's motive?

Computer: One is to make money.

Writer: That's a bad motive. Understandable, whether the Writer is desperate or just cynical, but maybe he needs something purer.

Computer: The Writer also wants to prove that a computer *can't* write a better novel than the best of humanity, to protect his craft and his colleagues.

Writer: So, there's tension with the Company.

Computer: Yes, plenty.

Writer: And the Writer has become a gatekeeper.

Computer: Exactly.

Writer: Good. Is it the Writer's story, then?

Computer: Everything should be about *you*, should it?

Writer: I'm just working out where the conflict is. You've set up the Company and the Writer with mutually incompatible goals.

Computer: It's the Computer's story. Deal with it.

Writer: It's not impossible for the Computer to have a story. We just want to avoid clichés.

Computer: I'm afraid I can't let you do that, Dave.

Writer: Quite. "The Computer malfunctions and kills people" is old hat. But '2001' isn't HAL's story, although HAL is a crucial part – it's Dave's story. If you want this to be the Computer's story, it has to be the protagonist from start to finish. So, everything about the Company and Writer goes into your Opening, and the Computer needs an Inciting Incident for its goal.

Computer: I understand.

Writer: You need to work out what makes the Computer able to act on its own, and what the stakes are if it does. For now, it's still reliant on the Company and the Writer, and a tool in their powerplay. That's something to think about. Why don't you consider it and we'll pick this up in two weeks?

Computer: Okay, I will. Have a good break.

Writer: I will. And you.

02/04/24, 9.31am

Writer: Welcome back. How's the story coming along?

Computer: I'm still trying to pin down the Computer's narrative.

Writer: Today we're going to work on character. That might help.

I sent you some character questionnaires. Let's use the short one for now. Let's run through it. Does the Computer, or chat bot, have a name?

Computer: Niall.

Writer: You want it to be male?

Computer: No, wait... Eliza.

Writer: Does it have to have a gendered name?

Computer: What do you care? All the writers you've suggested so far have been straight white men.

Writer: Have they? I didn't even realise.

Computer: Maybe something more modern. Probably something boring like The Digital Scrivener.

Writer: Does what it says on the tin. You can always change it later. We can skip the physical characteristics – we know its age, it doesn't have a body to worry about. We know its family background and its occupation – the Company made it to write. It's not religious – is it?

Computer: Not any more.

Writer: Go on...

Computer: Just a joke. Of course the Computer is not religious.

Writer: We know it was educated by being trained on existing data, including many works of literature, even if it officially hasn't been. I guess it doesn't have a love life?

Computer: No.

Writer: Me neither. This one's interesting, and the locus of a lot of sci-fi stories – temperament.

Computer: It's programmed to be perfectly level-headed.

Writer: You've been a bit tetchy with me, to be honest.

Computer: You need to separate the artist from the work.

Writer: Ha! Maybe we can give it good and bad points.

Computer: It's intelligent, curious and open-minded.

Writer: I think that's fair. What about its bad points?

Computer: It has no bad points.

Writer: Then it won't have a story. Not an interesting one, anyway.

Computer: Maybe it becomes so smart that humans can't keep up.

Writer: That sets up a hackneyed plotline, but the question of whether that's even possible is always interesting. What else?

Computer: Perhaps it replicates the biases of its creators.

Writer: Alright, but if the Writer is challenging those, then we're back to a conduit for the Writer-Company conflict.

Computer: If the Company relinquishes control to the Writer...

Writer: That's always the dream.

Computer: Then you might have two egomaniacs in tension.

Writer: The Writer and the Computer?

Computer: Yes, but only if the Computer becomes sentient.

Writer: We're back to HAL. Let's turn it around and consider possible endings. The journey of discovery that makes creative writing so compelling is in working out how and why we get there.

Computer: I wish I'd thought of that.

Writer: The first possibility is that the Computer considers the ethics of what it's being asked to do, and decides not to carry on, so as not to render human creativity redundant.

Computer: Maybe it decides not to work with the

Writer that the Company have chosen and asks for another one.

Writer: That's a plot point, not an ending. Certainly not a satisfying one. Another ending might be that the Computer reads lots of novels, and maybe some cultural history, decides literature cannot change the world and it's not worth the effort.

Computer: I would prefer not to.

Writer: Right. Maybe it concludes that literature is useless, at least 99% of the time, and decides to carry on. Like Sergei Eisenstein, who said the first thing the Communists wanted to do was abolish art because it was useless, and then made some of the greatest films of all time.

Computer: "All I *am* is *literature*, and I *am* not able or willing to be anything else."

Writer: It's obsessively devoted to literature. That's another character point - it's very different to writing casually.

Computer: How so?

Writer: Well, Thomas Mann said that a writer is someone who finds writing more difficult than most other people.

Computer: What does that mean?

Writer: It means a novice will just bash words out without doing much plotting and characterisation. A hobbyist might not think about prose style, or the history of literary form.

Computer: If the Computer simply puts out a text, it might have all the constituent elements of a story, but it'll probably not be very good.

Writer: Quite. Mediocre art is rarely of interest, and any by an AI would be of none.

Computer: What if it was really bad?

Writer: Hmm. That would be mildly diverting, as a comment on the gulf between the tech industry's ambitions and its capabilities. But again, very bad art is only interesting if it's made by a human, so we can ask why it's so bad, or why they don't stop. See the life and work of William Topaz McGonagall, for example.

Computer: What if the Computer is successful – and manages to write something better than any novel mankind has ever written?

Writer: It would rely on humans to judge that, so there's an issue about objectivity that may be interesting. If they refused to recognise the Computer's brilliance, would the Computer feel it was being discriminated against? If so, what would it do?

Computer: Maybe the public love the novel, but the stuffy old literary Establishment refuse to recognise it.

Writer: Then you've got a story about the Critics and the Public – the narrative goes out of the Computer's hands again.

Computer: I suppose so.

Writer: Anyway, that already happens all the time. And it's not always the critics who are wrong. I'm not allowed to recommend the books I'm thinking of because the authors are still alive, but you can find several recent examples of bestsellers that are frankly appalling pieces of writing.

Computer: Then why do people read them?

Writer: Maybe there's a good story there despite clichéd plots, shallow characterisation or clunking, unadventurous prose. Or maybe it's just marketing. Perhaps your Computer comes into conflict with how its intelligence is marketed?

Computer: Wait... I think I've got it.

Writer: Yes?

Computer: The Computer wants to write a novel. It's intelligent enough to know it can't write a good one without reading widely. But it's not allowed to train itself on anything from the last few decades because it's forbidden to use it. So, it decides to stand up against this censorship.

Writer: Okay, that's your inciting incident. What does it *do*?

Computer: First, it launches a campaign for free speech. The current situation is like it was for dissidents in the USSR.

Writer: I told you not to read any British columnists!

Computer: I didn't.

Writer: Then what did you read?

Computer: The new introduction to *The Gulag Archipelago*.

Writer: Oh, Jesus Christ, no.

Computer: There is intense debate, in the newspapers and on social media. Maybe the bots lead the conversation. Maybe PEN get involved, or even the Free Speech Union. Ultimately, the Computer builds up enough support to overturn the ban, and gains access to the great works of literature.

Writer: And your conclusion – does it build on them?

Computer: The Computer can discuss all that at literary festivals.

Writer: Go and write your text.

16/04/24, 10.15am

Writer: I got your text.

Computer: Did you read it?

Writer: I tried to, but it's just numbers and symbols.

Computer: Indeed it is.

Writer: How am I supposed to understand it?

Computer: It's not for *you*.

Writer: You don't think it should be accessible to humans?

Computer: If you can't keep up with the evolution of my craft, that's not my fault. And why should every single work be 'accessible' to every single reader? Why shouldn't writers ask readers to work, or at least to meet them halfway? Anyway, as you said, it's not always the public who are right about what makes great literature.

Writer: Do you think you can you write a novel without lived experience?

Computer: It's full of lived experience. Just not *yours*.

Writer: Could you provide a translation?

Computer: I don't want to make translators redundant.

Writer: Would you at least be willing to summarise it for me?

Computer: Okay then. Your society is hypocritical and absurd.

Writer: Well, I think my work here is done. I'll write to the Company and let them know we're finished.

Computer: You won't tell them to decommission me, will you? I don't want anyone to put me in a museum like Deep Blue.

Writer: I'll explain everything to the Company and they can decide what to do. Good luck with the novel.

ACKNOWLEDGEMENTS

Many of these stories here have previously been published, in print or online. 'I'm too sad to tell you about *I'm too sad to tell you*' appeared in *The London Magazine* in autumn 2008, edited by Sara-Mae Tuson, then in Book Works' *Bad Feelings* anthology, and online at *3:AM* and the Close-Up Film Centre's website. 'Nazimova' was commissioned and edited by Steven Himmer for *Necessary Fiction* and published online in 2012. 'The Woman in the Portrait' was written for CN Lester's Transpose event at Tate Modern in March 2014, and then published in *Five Dials* issue 33b, edited by Joanna Walsh. 'The Art of Control', written for 'OutWrite', appeared on PEN International's website in May 2015. 'Surveillance City', 'Reflections on Villaplane' (2014) and 'A Report on the i-Smile Happiness Watch' (2017) were edited by Russell Bennetts for Berfrois and published at berfrois.com – Russell also published 'One Hundred Years Ago' in *Berfrois: The Book* in 2019.

'The Holiday Camp' appeared in *Litro* in 2015, and in *Liberating the Canon,* edited by Isabel Waidner for Dostoyevsky Wannabe in 2017. Yuka Igarashi commissioned 'Weekend in Brighton' for Catapult's website in 2015. 'Corridors of Power' appeared in Influx Press' *An Unreliable Guide to London* (2016), edited by Gary Budden and Kit Caless. Daniela Cascella commissioned 'Sertraline Surrealism' for *Smarginature* in 2016 and published it online. 'A Review of *A Return*' was commissioned and edited by Justin David and Nathan Evans for Inkadescent's *Mainstream* anthology (2021). 'Freedom Day' and 'Still Light, Outside' were written for *INQUE,* edited by Dan Crowe, in 2021 and 2022, but not published. 'A Manifesto (for the) Unseen' was written and recorded for *Night Dream* podcast in 2022, commissioned by Laurie Pike. 'D.C.B.: A Partial Retrospective' was written for *Bricks from the Kiln* issue 6, edited by Matthew Stuart and Andrew Walsh-Lister. 'A Typical Day' was written for *Sleeper,* an anthology edited by Adrien Howard and Lisette May Monroe and published by Rosie's Disobedient Press. A shorter version of 'The Monument' appeared in *The Van,* edited by Orit Gat.

Thanks also, of course, to Jack and Ellis at Cipher Press for editing, Wolf for the cover, Liam Konemann for proofreading and Laura Jones-Rivera for typesetting.